Praise for

The Magdala League

Maggie was on a mission. It was one she had not anticipated. But since it involved an attack on her long-time friend, she did not hesitate to answer the call.

As she began her journey with her reliable friend Magersfontein, she soon saw again and again how God orchestrated whatever was needed to solve the secret of Captain Smith's house, even protecting her and her comrades as they sought to unravel the mystery. Interspersed throughout are a number of appetizing servings of food for both the body and the soul.

Once I started reading it, I could not put it down! And once I finished the book, I found that I had much to think about as I contemplated how my life, too, was planned by God.

—**Rev. Dr. Robert Bell**, chairman *of Collins Children's Home Board of Directors*; retired minister, former dean of *Erskine Theological Seminary*

***

Sarah Hicks has done a wonderful job putting together a book for youth that not only is entertaining and maintains one's interest, but also supplies a plethora of life lessons based upon Scripture. *The Magdala League: Mystery on Maple Street* will be a book that parents, grandparents, and others will enjoy reading to or sharing with their youngsters, with plenty of opportunities for discussion and learning together.

—**Alice**, pastor's wife, registered nurse

***

The Magdala League: Mystery on Maple Street is an enthralling Christian mystery that will captivate readers from the very first page. Following the journey of the spirited and inquisitive Maggie, this story is rich with intrigue, suspicion, and inspiration.

As Maggie navigates the twists and turns of her adventure, readers are not only entertained but also challenged to grow in their faith, and once I started reading it was hard to put it down.

This story stands out with its cool yet heart-warming style, offering a fresh and exciting perspective that is often lacking in today's Christian media. It is a must-read for anyone seeking a compelling story that both thrills and uplifts. It is sure to captivate every reader that embarks on this journey in *The Magdala League: Mystery on Maple Street.*

—**Pastor Kerry and First Lady Leslie Boone**, Crosspoint Church of *El Paso*

The Magdala League: Mystery on Maple Street

Happy reading

Sarah L Hicks

by

S. L. Hicks

Published by KHARIS PUBLISHING, an imprint of
KHARIS MEDIA LLC.

Copyright © 2024 S. L Hicks

ISBN-13: 978-1-63746-265-2
ISBN-10: 1-63746-265-4

Library of Congress Control Number:

All KHARIS PUBLISHING products are available at special
quantity discounts for bulk purchase for sales promotions,
premiums, fund-raising, and educational needs. For details,
contact:

Kharis Media LLC
Tel: 1-630-909-3405
support@kharispublishing.com
www.kharispublishing.com

Soli Deo gloria. In memory of my grandmother, Irene, who inspired my love of adventure and mystery, and to my husband, Jeff, for his undaunted belief in me.

CONTENTS

Chapter I: Mystery on Maple Street...................................... 11

Chapter II: Shadrach and Meshach 19

Chapter III: Deed Searching with Dodie........................... 27

Chapter IV: Waylaying Mr. Weyer..................................... 35

Chapter V: A Game Plan Over Gashouse Eggs 43

Chapter VI: Subterfuge on Chamberlain Avenue............. 51

Chapter VII: The Real McCoy 59

Chapter VIII: The Magdala League Explained.................. 67

Chapter IX: Pizza, Pie, and Providence.............................. 75

Chapter X: A Tall Ship with a Tall Tale.............................. 83

Chapter XI: The Flags' Message 91

Chapter XII: Liaison Over Lasagna 99

Chapter XIII: The Maple Street Gang............................... 107

Chapter XIV: The Feller in the Cellar............................... 115

Chapter XV: A Puzzle in Plain Sight................................. 123

Chapter XVI: The Secret Under the Stairs........................ 131

Chapter XVII: Mary's Homecoming.................................. 141

Chapter XVIII: Rolling it up at the Rink.......................... 149

Chapter

1

MYSTERY ON MAPLE STREET

"Ahh," said the thinnish, middle-aged woman standing by the gas pump and stretching her arms and legs. With only fifteen more miles to go, she was eager to finish her journey. She removed the gas cap from her motorcycle, lifted the gasoline nozzle, and flipped the lever to turn on the pump. The needle on her bike's fuel gauge was ever so close to empty, so she thought it best to fill up now. *I'm not sure what to expect when I get to Mary's house.* Within a minute or two, the tank was full. She replaced the cap and nozzle and then walked inside the station building.

"Good afternoon," said a young man behind the counter.

"Good afternoon. That's me on the far side." The attendant glanced at a control panel at his right.

"The far side. Like the comic," he laughed. The woman smiled.

"Unintentional pun, but they are funny comics."

11

"That will be two dollars and ninety cents, please. My favorite so far is the caveman wanting pasta instead of going hunting."

She handed the clerk three dollars and said, "I've seen that one. I'm with the caveman. You can't go wrong with pasta." Glancing at the counter, she noticed a rectangular daily calendar. "Is it the fourth already?"

"Yes, it is." He cleared his throat. "There will never be another Monday, June 4, 1984," he said in a deep voice. "That's how my history professor puts it," he laughed.

"That's very true. Say, you wouldn't happen to have any fresh coffee?"

"Well, not exactly fresh. I made it about two hours ago, but you're welcome to it. I'll have to discard it soon anyway." The young man put his hand across the counter to return a dime for change.

"No, no, you keep it. I just appreciate the coffee."

"Have you come from a long way away?"

"Yes, I guess you could say that. I'm unsure of the mileage, but I left the Midwest on Saturday afternoon."

"Wow! You've made good time! Say, how does that outfit ride?"

The two glanced out the large front window at the motorcycle beside the pump. She smiled and said, "It's great. And you can't beat the storage space in the sidecar."

By this time, she had poured what was left of the coffee into a small white foam cup and was sipping happily from it. "Mmm, hot coffee! I'm Maggie, by the way, Maggie North," she said, extending her hand across the counter.

"Brad Davis," said the young man. He returned a firm handshake.

"Related to—?" she asked, pointing to a sign on the store's back wall.

The young man lightly laughed. "Yes, that's my grandfather. I help out between classes and during summer break."

"I know he appreciates it. So, you're in college?"

"Yes. Studying architecture."

"How interesting!"

"Well, I'm only into my second year, but I'm hooked!"

Maggie swallowed the final sip of coffee and then tossed the cup into a nearby trashcan. "Well, Brad, it was a pleasure to meet you, and I wish you well with your studies."

"Thanks, and have a safe trip."

"Thank you," she replied, pushing through the glass door. Maggie breathed in the sweet-smelling air. *That's lilac, I think.* She spotted a deep purple lilac bush just off the paved lot beside a wooden picnic table. She strolled toward her bike, enjoying the fragrance and thanking God for the beauty of his creation.

Maggie sat astride the bike and then started the engine. She paused to enjoy the soft rumbling, saying aloud, "And we'll work in an oil change and service for you, Magers, once things get sorted." She lovingly patted the bike's gas tank and then pulled on her helmet and gloves. With a roar of the engine, she headed back onto the two-lane road.

The area was rural, with houses few and far between. The bucolic scenery was so beautiful that viewing it from the openness of her bike made the fifteen miles go by quickly. Soon, the town limit sign came into view. It was painted a tasteful shade of green with gold paint highlighting the carved lettering, which read: "Kevan's Cove, established 1864, population 2,438."

Hello again, Kevan's Cove. Growing, I see. Your population is up by about fifty since I was last here. She rode down the town's main street, slowing a bit to read the road signs. *Elm, Magnolia, Walnut. Aha, Maple!* She turned right onto a narrow road. *And Mary's house should be coming up soon. Yep, there it is.* With that thought, Maggie turned the bike into the driveway of a small, two-story house. She parked under a detached carport and shut off the engine.

"Thank you, Lord, for the safe journey. Please guide me in all that needs to be done here," she prayed as she released her helmet clasp. She glanced around the property. Not much had changed since her last visit. The blue paint on the house siding was a little faded, as was the white picket fence. The lawn, a one-acre lot, was neatly mown. She turned as the house's screen door slowly squeaked open, and a young man of about sixteen peered around the door edge.

"Hello, Monk. I'm Maggie North." At saying this, the woman dismounted the bike, removed her gloves, and then walked toward the door with her right hand extended. The young man looked relieved and clasped her hand with a careful handshake. She said, "You and I have a bit to do today. Do you mind helping me carry in a few things?"

Monk left the doorway and walked to the drive. He stood still for a moment, admiring the motorcycle.

"Ah, I see you like Magersfontein," said Maggie as she lifted the backrest of the sidecar and removed two duffle bags. She stowed her helmet before closing the compartment. "Magers and I have traveled quite a few miles together. He's a good bike!" Handing Monk a duffel bag, Maggie said, "Let's get these inside."

Monk led the way through the door and into a cozy kitchen. The white paint on the walls and wooden cabinets lent light to the room as the sun beamed brightly through the large windows.

"This was always my favorite room. Bright, warm, and so many delicious smells," remembered Maggie as she and Monk placed the duffle bags onto the seats of two chairs alongside the wooden kitchen table. Maggie removed her leather jacket and swung it on the back of one of the chairs. "How is she today, Monk?"

Though tall and ruddy, Monk was quiet, his shyness earning him his nickname. He breathed before answering Maggie. "Well, she's awake. The doctor wants to keep her for the rest of the week."

"I think that's best," Maggie said. It gives us time to do a little sleuthing. Are you up to helping me?"

A large grin appeared on the boy's face. There weren't many adventures to be had in Kevan's Cove, so the prospect of a bit of excitement was always welcome.

"What can you tell me about the attack on Mary?"

"Not a lot. I was at the youth group meeting at church when it happened. When I came home, Mary was lying on the living room floor unconscious. She had blood on the back of her head. The police haven't said a lot. Honestly, I don't think they have a suspect."

"I see. It sounds like she surprised the intruder. Was she supposed to be at home?"

"Well, that's the thing. No. She usually goes to read to old Mrs. Wainwright down the street, but Mrs. Wainwright's family was in town to visit, so Mary stayed home."

"Hmm. I'm a little road-weary, but now is not the time to rest." She stood and said, "There is still a genuine threat of danger, and we must be prepared for a visitor tonight. I think, my dear Monk, that it is time to visit the honorable Reverend McPherson." She moved to the kitchen door and continued, "Let's take the back way."

Maggie and Monk exited through the door, ensuring it was securely locked. They walked through a narrow gap in the backyard hedge and then onto the sidewalk of a neighboring street.

Jim McPherson was Maggie's longtime friend. Their paths had crossed on missionary trips, church postings, and travel excursions. At sixty-five, the pastor was now serving at the small community church. Maggie and Monk walked about a block and then turned left. The old church building came into view.

It may be old, Maggie thought, *but I love the beauty of that large, white steeple, long stained-glass windows and rock foundation.*

They followed a small sidewalk between the church building and the manse. Just as Maggie raised her hand to lift the brass doorknocker, the door swung open, and a white-haired, cheery-faced man exclaimed, "Maggie North! As I live and breathe!"

Chapter

II

SHADRACH AND MESHACH

"**C**ome in, come in! How in the world are you, Miss North?"

"I'm as right as rain on a hot August day! How about you?" Looking around the room, she continued, "This is a slower pace for you."

"Ah, that it is, but it suits me. Right now, it's where God wants me to be."

The two paused momentarily and reflected on the peace that comes from obedience to God. Maggie remembered the struggles and stress of fighting against the story God wrote for her. *Life only really begins when you live for God.*

"I can read your thoughts," jested Reverend Jim. "Well, at the very least, I've been there."

"Changing the subject," Maggie said, "I believe you know Monk?"

"Hello, Pastor," said Monk in a quiet voice.

"Yes, I keep a watchful eye on this one. He's special."

Smiling, she said, "I believe you. You know why I'm here?"

"Yes. They're out back and well in need of a little excursion. They tend to get restless in this quiet community."

"Excellent. I think we could all use a little adventure," responded Maggie.

Reverend Jim led the way through the small manse to the backyard. "Shadrach, Meshach, come." At this, two very large and powerful Dobermans bounded to the back stoop. At the sight of Maggie and Monk, their short tails wagged frantically from side to side.

"Why hello, fellas! It's been a while." Maggie greeted the lads, rubbing their heads and scratching behind their ears. Monk, quickly losing his shyness, followed suit.

"Still the same commands?" asked Maggie.

"Yes, but they've added an important one to their repertoire." Turning to the lads, Jim said, "Shadrach, Meshach. Guard!"

Straight away, the two lads began growling and baring their teeth while encircling the terrified Monk. "Lads. At ease." Immediately, they resumed their cheerful demeanors.

"Again, excellent, Jim," Maggie said, stepping aside with him while Monk continued playing with Shadrach and Meshach.

"How much do you know?" asked Reverend Jim.

"Saturday morning, I received a call from headquarters while on a job in the Midwest. They said Mary had been attacked late Friday evening. All they knew was that it was due to a break-in. Mary was taken to the hospital, but besides being told she was stable, that's all they knew. Needless to say, I came straight here. Monk said it wasn't her normal pattern to be home on Friday evenings, which means she surprised the prowler. What could Mary possibly have that would be worth attacking her for?"

"Well," began Reverend Jim, "let me fill you in on the rest of the story. Mary came to me about a week ago, worried about becoming forgetful. She noticed things in the house, small things, shifted from their usual position. Then, on Thursday, she returned home from the grocery store and found the back door wide open. It became clear at this point that Mary wasn't suffering from dementia. She was planning to have an alarm system installed, but the attack happened and, well, you know the rest."

"It just doesn't make any sense. We Magdalas don't have anything of worldly value. Following the tradition of our founder, everything is used to further the message of Christ."

"I've been thinking about that. I am not convinced that it's something Mary owns. There could be something of value in the house that was placed there long before she moved in."

"I think I understand. You mean that to begin unraveling this mystery, we must first find out more about the house."

"Yes, I think that's the place to start."

"Well then, there's no time like the present." Turning to look at the teen and the lads, Maggie continued, "And how is Monk? Mary said he still wasn't talking much."

Smiling, the pastor replied, "Well, Monk never was one for a whole lot of words, but I think he is still working through the death of his aunt. As you know, she took him in after his parents were killed in Brazil."

"Yes, I remember." Maggie paused. "I remember all of that like it was yesterday."

"I'm sorry. I didn't mean to bring that up."

"No, it's okay. I often think about Madeline and Ben and their work in Brazil. It just all ended so sadly."

"You've been quite a few places, haven't you, Maggie?"

"Yes, but not for very long. There is always another mission lined up."

"I know," said Jim. "Well, I'm glad you were sent to help with this. You are just the one for the job."

"'I can do everything through him who gives me strength' (Philippians 4:13)."

"Well put, my dear. We are all here by his design, and he does indeed strengthen and guide us. And Monk's faith is strong. He just has a quiet nature."

"Madeline was the same. There was a whole lot going on upstairs, but very few words made their way out."

"And Monk seems to be taking after his mother."

"Well, thanks again for the loan of the lads. Keep us in your prayers tonight!" With this, Maggie returned to Monk and then tapped him on the shoulder. "Have a go at giving them a command."

In a not-so-timid voice, Monk said, "Shadrach, Meshach. Sit!" A sudden confidence appeared in the young man. Maggie looked knowingly at Reverend Jim.

He's right, as always. Monk will be just fine. Reverend Jim handed Monk two red leather leashes, which he attached to the lads' collars.

"And here is their 'doggie bag,'" he laughed, handing her a brown paper bag.

"I'll see you tomorrow morning, then?"

"Tomorrow it is! Have plenty of coffee, and some breakfast would be nice."

She laughed and replied, "Sure thing." Turning to Monk, she said, "Shall we go?"

Monk nodded in agreement, and off they walked down the block. "I think it best if we keep the presence of Shadrach and Meshach a surprise, don't you?" Monk, again, nodded in agreement. "Then, let us return from whence we came."

Once back at Mary's house, Monk stayed with the lads while Maggie stealthily opened the backdoor. She then motioned to Monk. Quickly and quietly, all entered the house.

"I don't think our prowler will try again until dark. That gives us a little bit of time. Why don't we do some research?" Monk's face lit up. "Alright then! Let's get Shadrach and Meshach comfortable first." Monk removed bowls and dog food from the bag Reverend Jim had sent along with them. After filling the bowls with water and food, he replaced the dog food and then tucked the bag into a cabinet.

"Alright, lads," said Maggie, looking at the Dobermans, "be on your best behavior." The two dogs, thirsty from their exercise, contentedly lapped water from the bowls.

"I didn't know that Shadrach and Meshach were that well-trained," Monk said in a surprised tone. I mean, they act like normal dogs."

Laughing, Maggie replied, "Yes. Reverend Jim is just full of surprises. He trained them himself you know."

"What? I didn't know he could do that?"

"Yes, it is just one of his many little hobbies. Now, will you give me directions to the courthouse?"

"Yes."

"Good. It will be closing soon, so we'll start there first."

Maggie and Monk exited again by the back door and then headed to the carport. "Are you okay with riding in the sidecar?" Monk, again, smiled. "Fine." She paused, "I'm just curious. Have you ever ridden a motorcycle before?"

"Yes, my uncle John had one similar to Magersfontein. He taught me how to ride when he was visiting last summer. I just passed the test a few months ago and got my license."

"Most excellent," replied Maggie. "You don't have one of your own yet?"

Monk's face looked downcast. "I've had a little difficulty convincing Miss Mary."

"Say no more. I know how she is. It would be convenient for you, though, to have a bike, especially when you start college. Have you decided what you want to study?"

"No, not really. May I ask you something?"

"Ask away."

"How did you come to do what you do now?"

"Ha, how much time do you have for that story?"

"I guess what I mean," explained Monk further, "is how do I know what God wants me to do?"

Maggie paused a moment to reflect. "I'm not one for career advice. You can ask Miss Mary about that later. However, I think it is important as Christians to remember why we are here in this fallen world. Before Jesus left this earth, he said, 'Therefore go and make disciples of all nations, baptising them in the name of the Father and of the Son and of the Holy Spirit, and teaching them to obey everything I have commanded you. And surely I am with you always, to the very end of the age' (Matthew 28:19-20). That is the Great Commission. That is our real job, our real purpose. I believe God gives us vocations here to facilitate

S. L. Hicks

spreading his Message. In Psalms 139:15-16, God tells us that he has already written our life's story. He will lead us. We have to trust him. You'll know what to do when it's time to make that decision." Monk smiled. Then Maggie added, "But as to how I came to do what I do, well, that's a story for another time."

She retrieved her helmet from the storage bin behind the sidecar seatback. After fastening the chin strap, she reached into the sidecar's footwell. Handing Monk a helmet, she said, "Here you go. Buckle up, and we'll be off!"

Chapter

III

DEED SEARCHING WITH DODIE

Magersfontein popped and purred as the two rode into the heart of Kevan's Cove. Using hand signals, Monk directed Maggie to the courthouse. Like most small towns, it was in the center and easy to find. Maggie quickly located a parking space, and the two alighted and then headed inside.

"Hello," Maggie said to the clerk at the front desk. We're interested in searching for a deed."

"Upstairs, second door on the left."

"Thank you." Maggie and Monk walked left toward the staircase and then proceeded up the steps. The worn tread squeaked softly under their footsteps. At the top, they entered the second door as directed.

"How may I help you?" asked a young woman. Maggie, guessing she was about sixteen, surmised that this was probably a summer job for her. "Oh, hi, Monk! I didn't see you. How are you?"

Monk smiled, but his face began reddening. "Hello, Dodie," he replied.

Maggie smiled knowingly and asked Dodie about conducting a deed search.

"Yes, I can help you with that. What is the property address?"

"412 Maple Avenue."

"Miss Mary's property? Yes, I have the records right here. You know, y'all aren't the first to ask about the deed history."

"Oh, is that right?"

"Yes, a stranger was in here a little while back. He wanted a complete history of the ownership of that property. I wrote it all down. Fortunately, I made an extra copy because it seemed a little odd to me. But, you know, public records and all."

Monk asked Dodie, "Can you describe him?"

"Tallish, late thirties, dirty blond hair, somewhat muscular. And rude! He just grabbed the paper from my hand and left without so much as a thank-you. Oh, and he had a weird kind of scar on his left hand. Like a bullet wound. It looked like one my Uncle John had from when he was shot in Korea."

"Dodie, you are a gem!" exclaimed Maggie. "You must come over for dinner soon."

Dodie smiled at Monk as she handed Maggie the deed history. "Thank you. I would love to."

"Thanks a bunch," said Maggie.

"Bye, Monk."

"Bye, Dodie." Maggie and Monk exited through the door, headed down the creaking stairs, and then out the courthouse door.

"Dodie," Maggie said with a tone of raillery, "she seems like just your type." Monk quickly put on the helmet to cover his blushing face. "I shouldn't tease you. But honestly, Dodie is a very nice girl, and this excursion has been most profitable. Let's keep this for later when we have more time to look over it." She tucked the document inside her jacket. Now, I need directions to the historical society."

"It's combined with the town museum. It's on Fourth Street, I think."

"Kevan's Cove has a museum? Wow! This town is moving up in the world," laughed Maggie as she took her seat and started the bike's engine. Monk slid into the sidecar. Magersfontein roared to life, and the two exited the parking lot and rode a few blocks down, turning onto Fourth Street. A rather large sign on the building's front identified the site. Maggie pulled into an empty parking spot in front, and then the two entered the building.

"Good afternoon, and welcome to Kevan's Cove. My name is Patricia Blakey, but you can call me Pat," said a short, enthusiastic woman. "How may I help you?"

"Thank you," replied Maggie. "I'm new to the area and was searching for a book about the history of the local houses."

"Well, then you are in for a treat! We just received copies of a book published by our local historian, Erasmus Beauregard. We affectionately call him Uncle Ras." She continued as she held up a copy of the book, "Most of the more prominent homes are featured. Are you staying locally?"

"Yes, I'm a friend of Miss Mary."

"Oh, my. What a shock we all had when we heard what happened to Mary. This has always been such a quiet town. We've never had anything like that happen before."

"Yes, Monk and I were also shocked."

"How is she doing?"

Monk replied, "The doctors want to keep her for observation. She received a pretty strong blow to the head."

"She's in my prayers. You'll let her know, won't you?"

"Yes, we will, Pat," said Maggie, "and we'll take a copy of Mr. Beauregard's book."

Pat made her way to a desk in the corner of the room, took out a sales booklet, and then hand-wrote a receipt. "That will be ten dollars and a quarter."

Maggie handed her the exact change. Pat placed the book in a brown paper bag and then handed it across the desk. "Well, enjoy the book, and welcome to Kevan's Cove. If you're here next week, be sure to visit our newest exhibit. It's on the pirates of Kevan's Cove."

"I didn't know pirates frequented Kevan's Cove. How interesting," Maggie mused. "Well, thank you, Pat."

Back outside, Maggie scanned the surrounding buildings. "I missed lunch, and we won't have time to fix dinner. Is there any place to get a quick bite to eat?" she asked Monk.

"The Corner Grill is just over there," he said, motioning to a small storefront. "It's nothing special, but the food is good."

"It looks like a delectable dive to me. How are the fries?"

"They're delicious."

The two walked a short distance to the restaurant. Monk opened the door, and a small bell rang out. They entered and then seated themselves at the counter. The circular stools were a little worse for the wear, but everything was clean.

"What can I get ya?" asked a blonde-haired woman with numerous pencils behind her ears. Her eyes were focused on a well-used order pad in her hand. She continued as she looked up, "Oh, hey, Monk!"

"Hi, Doreen."

"The usual for you?"

"Yes, ma'am."

"What's your usual?" whispered Maggie.

"A burger with fries and a chocolate shake," he smiled.

Maggie said, "Ditto the fries for me, but how about a grilled cheese sandwich and a strawberry shake?"

"We can do that. I'll have your order out shortly." Doreen continued to write as she turned toward the kitchen pass-through. She called out, "Hey, Pete. Order up." Just then, the bell on the glass door rang again.

"Hey, Monk!"

Monk turned around to the older gentleman who had greeted him.

"Maggie, this is my neighbor, Mr. Butler. Mr. Butler, Maggie North."

"Pleasure to meet you," said Mr. Butler. "Mind if I join y'all?"

"Please do," said Maggie.

"I've been meaning to say something to you, Monk. I've been trying to keep an eye out since Miss Mary's attack. I noticed an orange sportscar driving past your house for the last few evenings. It slowly coasts by. If the lights are on, it drives off. But, if everything is dark, the car pulls off onto a backstreet. That's all I can see from my front window."

"Wow, Mr. Butler! I'm impressed," said Maggie. "Thank you. That information is extremely helpful." Turning to the counter, she said, "Doreen, whatever Mr. Butler wants, put it on my bill."

"You don't have to do that."

"I do, and I will."

"The usual?" asked Doreen.

"The usual, please," replied Mr. Butler. Turning again to Maggie and Monk, he continued. "Are you staying at Miss Mary's house?"

"Yes. I just got into town—."

"A few hours ago," continued Mr. Butler.

"You really don't miss much from the window of yours."

"No, ma'am, I don't. That's a nice bike. That's how I knew you were here. Not many sidecar outfits in Kevan's Cove."

Maggie smiled. "About what time does that car drive by the house?"

"Well, it's usually between eight and nine-thirty. The tags are from out of state, New Jersey."

Doreen set down three plates of food and three milkshakes. "I'm partial to the chocolate, too," said Mr. Butler to Monk, who smiled as he sipped from the tall, frosty glass before him.

"Oh, it must be good. I can tell from the expression on his face," laughed Maggie.

"My dear," replied Mr. Butler, "this is some of the finest fare in Kevan's Cove." The threesome continued to chat while enjoying the food. After they finished, Maggie and Monk slid off the counter stools.

"It was a real pleasure to meet you, Mr. Butler. And thanks again for the information."

"I'll see you around." He paused, then continued, "Hey Monk, let Miss Mary know I'm keeping an eye out."

"I will, Mr. Butler, and thank you." Maggie and Monk left the diner and then returned to the bike.

"Mr. Butler is a Godsend," said Maggie. "Now we know when to expect our intruder AND what kind of car he drives. That is extremely helpful."

Back on the bike, Maggie started the engine while Monk hopped into the sidecar. They were soon back on the road and headed home to Maple Street.

Chapter

IV

WAYLAYING MR. WEYER

Maggie and Monk sat at the kitchen table, planning the evening's events. "I'm certain he'll try to break in again because whatever he is after is still in the house. So, our first course of action is to put our prowler out of commission, so to speak."

"What do you need me to do?" asked Monk.

Maggie replied, "I don't think we need to engage our mystery guest directly. You stay with the lads and watch for a signal."

"What's the signal?"

"You'll know it when you see it. When you do, command the lads to guard, just like Reverend Jim did this afternoon."

"Got it. Where will you be?"

"Where I have good aim." Monk looked confused. Maggie continued, "I can't explain all of my plan now, but trust me and remember, God is for us. In fact, let's pray for wisdom and protection." The two bowed their heads. "Father, thank you for taking such good care of us. Please heal Mary quickly so that she may be here with us soon. Thank you for the information we found today, and thank you for Mr. Butler. Be our light in the darkness of this evening as we go to battle in your name. We acknowledge your sovereignty in everything and rest in your care. Amen."

"Amen," added Monk. "Back to my earlier question, what exactly do you do? Miss Mary has read me excerpts from your letters describing your adventures. It seems that you've traveled quite a bit."

"Yes. I do love a good adventure. Tell me, Monk, how much do you know about Mary?"

"I know she is a Christian and sincerely cares about others."

"To me, Mary has always been an example of Jesus' love," Maggie said, pausing before she continued, "What I am about to tell you is not common knowledge, meaning it isn't something that is known by everyone in town, or all the little towns throughout the country. Please remember that."

"I understand," said Monk.

"Miss Mary and I are members of an organization with its roots in Christ's ministry. It's called the Magdala League, named after Mary of Magdala. As you know, she was an early follower of Christ. Jesus healed her and many other women. Because of their love and devotion to him, they financed his ministry. Luke 8 tells us that these women traveled with Jesus and were counted among his disciples. And that, in a nutshell, is what we still do today. A good portion of our work remains financial, but we also come alongside others, when needed, to assist in other areas. I am in the 'other areas' department."

"So, Reverend Jim, that is how you and Miss Mary know him?" queried Monk.

"Yes, he has enlisted the help of the Magdala League a few times." She paused, then continued, "That's also how I knew your mother, Madeline."

"You knew my mother?" Monk said eagerly. "Was she part of the Magdala League?"

"Yes. She was a Magdala, and I promise I will tell you the rest of the story but," she said, glancing at the wall clock, "it will have to wait. We need to put out the lights and pretend to leave. It's almost eight o'clock." Monk reluctantly agreed.

"I think we'll leave only one table lamp on. That will provide just enough light. Take the lads and leave them in the back bedroom. We'll walk out the front door, down the block until we're out of sight, then sneak in through the back hedge."

Monk gave a thumbs-up as he led Shadrach and Meshach away to their assigned post. He quickly returned. Together, they opened the front door wide, conspicuously locked it, walked down the driveway, and then onto the sidewalk. "Now, in case we are being watched, we need to look the part, so let's keep up a conversation."

As planned, the two continued down the sidewalk a few blocks and then turned onto a side street.

Ensuring no cars were parked within sight, they ducked into a nearby backyard. Stealthily going from yard to yard, the two returned to the hedge around Miss Mary's backyard. They stepped through the narrow gap and quietly entered the house unseen.

"Now to our posts," said Maggie. Monk joined Shadrach and Meshach in the back bedroom while Maggie concealed herself behind a large armchair in the front room. She could hear the ticking of the kitchen clock. A half-hour dragged slowly by. Suddenly, she heard metal scraping on the backdoor lock. *Here we go,* she thought, as the lock clicked and the door slowly creaked open.

The intruder passed through the kitchen and into the front room, where the solitary table lamp illuminated his profile. Leaning out from behind the chair, Maggie quietly raised a small blowgun to her mouth and then carefully blew into it. Within seconds, there was a loud bang as the intruder's body hit the floor. Monk and the lads excitedly entered the room.

"Guard!" ordered Monk. The lads obediently began circling the man. "Is he dead?"

"No, not dead. He's conscious, just temporarily immobilized. A little curare goes a long way." She knelt near the body and carefully removed a small dart. "Let's get him tied up before it wears off." Monk retrieved some strong rope from the utility closet in the hallway, and then together, he and Maggie securely trussed up the stranger.

"Look," said Maggie, pointing to the stranger's left hand, "here's the scar, just like Dodie described." She tied an extra knot in the rope. "And for good measure—" Maggie removed a blue bandana from her jacket pocket and stuffed it in the man's mouth. Carefully checking his pockets, she retrieved a wallet, a ring of keys, and several scraps of paper. After examining the wallet's contents, Maggie began, "Well, Mr. Donovan Weyer, we've got you now. Monk, call the police. Oh, and when they get here, let's not mention the blowgun to them, okay? They may not understand." Monk smiled and nodded in agreement as Maggie continued, "I'm going to find Mr. Weyer's car and see what clues it holds."

Maggie exited through the backdoor to the drive and then followed the sidewalk to the next corner. With little effort, she found an orange sportscar clumsily hidden down a backstreet. Using the rectangular key from the marked set, she opened the passenger door and pushed the button to release the glove compartment. She noted, "Registration, repair invoice, hotel matchbook, restaurant and gas receipts." She moved a paper closer to the cab light. "Keeping track of your time, hmm? So, it seems you were working for someone else." Maggie replaced the contents, closed the glove compartment, and slid out. She walked to the back of the vehicle and opened the boot, noting, "Not much here, and it's almost time for the police."

Maggie returned to the house. Before she replaced the intruder's wallet, she carefully wrote down the address from his driver's license and the one from an apartment complex business card. She tucked the paper slips into her back pocket. The intruder groaned slightly, causing the lads to increase their pace and growl. As if on cue, they heard a police siren—faint at first, then gradually becoming louder and louder.

Finally, a police car pulled into the driveway, and two uniformed officers rushed through the front door. Unprepared for what they encountered, the older of the two slowly began to speak. "Um, there was a report of a break-in at this address?"

"Yes, officer, here is the intruder," said Maggie. "Lads. At ease." Shadrach and Meshach immediately ceased their guard command and quietly sat down, staring intently at the two officers.

"How did you—" began the other officer. Maggie quickly interrupted, "I think he must have become paralyzed with fear. He just fell. The lads here did all the work. We just tied him up." She gave Monk a quick smile.

The officers placed handcuffs on Donovan Weyer before removing the rope that bound him. The younger officer bundled it up, handed it to Monk, and then escorted the groggy intruder to the patrol car. At the same time, Maggie efficiently answered the questions of the older policeman.

"I think that is all we need for now," he said. "We'll let you know if we have more questions."

"Thank you," said Maggie. While waiting at the door as the officers left the driveway, Maggie waved across the street to Mr. Butler's house. Light suddenly poured from the distant window, illuminating the figure of Mr. Butler waving back. Maggie closed and then locked the front door.

Chapter

V

A Game Plan
Over Gashouse Eggs

"I think we've earned some late-night cocoa, don't you?" Maggie asked as she entered the kitchen.

"That went pretty well," managed Monk.

"You know, Monk, God was looking out for us. I've never had that clean of a shot with the blow gun."

Maggie went to the pantry and removed a glass canning jar filled to the brim with the powdery goodness that was Miss Mary's secret hot cocoa mix. "Oh, how I have missed this." After filling the kettle from the stovetop with water, she placed it on a burner and then lit the gas.

"So, what's next?" asked Monk.

"I think we'll visit Mr. Weyer's residence tomorrow. I have his keyring." Monk looked a little concerned, but Maggie said, "I know, I know, but if I gave it to the police straight off, we might miss some important clues. They're only concerned about the break-in and Miss Mary's attack, whereas we are looking for the why. Besides, I'll drop it by the station on our way back. Right now, we need to get to the bottom of this mystery to ensure that Mary stays safe in this house once she's back home." Monk nodded in agreement.

The kettle emitted a soft whistle. Maggie clicked off the burner while Monk took two green glass mugs from the cabinet and spoons from a nearby drawer. He carefully spooned three scoops of the mixture into each mug, and Maggie filled them with boiling water. She and Monk sat down again at the table, thoughtfully stirring their cocoa. Maggie was the first to take a sip. "Mmm. A hint of heat from the chili pepper. Absolutely delicious!"

"Curare?" Monk said.

"Yes, it's a poison made from the *chondrodendron tomentosum* plant. It has to pierce the skin and enter the bloodstream for its paralyzing effects to occur. Ingesting it or skin contact don't work. I learned how to use it in South America. You know, the blowgun is quite an efficient weapon. Very stealthy."

"After tonight, I believe you!" The two sipped contentedly while Shadrach and Meshach stretched out on the kitchen floor.

Maggie was the first to finish her cocoa. Rising from her chair, she said, "I'll let the lads out, and then it's time for bed. Tomorrow is going to be busy." She whistled for the dogs and opened the back door. The two Dobermans obediently exited to the backyard.

"I'm beginning to understand what you were talking about earlier," Monk said. "It isn't so much worrying about my purpose in this world. God has already given that to me. It's about accepting and living the story he wrote for me."

"That's right, Monk. God is in control. Just trust him!" Shadrach and Meshach, tired from the night's activities, quickly whined at the backdoor. Maggie opened it wide, and they returned inside. She rinsed out the two mugs and then clicked off the kitchen light.

"Well, the doors are locked, and I'm exhausted. I'll wash up and then crash on the couch tonight."

As Monk headed upstairs, he turned and said, "Goodnight, Maggie. Thanks for coming."

"Goodnight, Monk, and you are most welcome."

The night came and went and was, thankfully, very uneventful after the capture of Mr. Weyer. Maggie rose early, as was her habit, and after washing up, she changed from her pink pajamas to a black crew-neck t-shirt and jeans. She started the coffee percolating on the old gas stove. It was still dark, but a bird chirped happily outside the kitchen window.

Maggie spread out her well-worn leather Bible on the kitchen table. She read aloud, "'Hear, O Israel, today you are going into battle against your enemies. Do not be faint-hearted or afraid; do not be terrified or give way to panic before them. For the LORD your God is the one who goes with you to fight for you against your enemies to give you victory' (Deuteronomy 20:3-4). Father, thank you for last night's victory. I pray these words again as I ask you to keep Monk and me from being faint-hearted. Lead our steps today, protect us as we investigate, and go before us, preparing the way to victory. I ask that you uncover this evil so Mary may be safe again as she serves you in this community."

The coffee began to bubble softly in the percolator. Maggie sat in the stillness, meditating on God's Word and listening to his guidance. The dark sky began softly transforming into a violet hue, anticipating the rising sun. Shadrach and Meshach slowly peered around the doorway, their eyes squinting from the kitchen light.

"Good morning, lads," she said with a smile. She patted their heads and moved to the back door. She opened it and then motioned for them to go out into the backyard, which they did with pleasure. She watched from the window as they sniffed different areas, still detecting scents from last night's events. All at once, their ears perked up, and they began running toward the back hedge.

It must be Reverend Jim. Opening the door, Maggie said, "The coffee is percolating."

"Just the way I like it. So, how did last night go? I was praying."

"I can always count on your prayers. It went very well. 'The horse is made ready for the day of battle, but victory rests with the LORD' (Proverbs 21:31). He definitely was with us last night."

"Hallelujah and amen!"

At this point, Monk entered the kitchen, yawning sleepily. "Good morning," he said, quietly sitting at the table.

"Good morning," said Reverend Jim and Maggie in unison.

"How about some gashouse eggs?" asked Maggie.

"Gashouse what?"

"The German is *Gasthaus*, meaning an inn, but it is known as *gashouse* here in the States." As Maggie began preparing the food, Reverend Jim poured Monk a cup of coffee. The teen breathed in the intoxicating smell. "I know, right?" said Maggie. "Nothing says 'Morning!' like a cup of hot coffee!"

"Now, my dear, on to the details of last night," continued Reverend Jim.

"She shot him with curare," said Monk excitedly. "Then he just fell over."

"It made for an easy capture," laughed Maggie.

"From your time in South America?"

Maggie nodded. "I looked through his pockets before the police came. He's living in an apartment here in Kevan's Cove."

"Do you think he's acting alone?"

Maggie paused before responding. "No, I don't. There were receipts and a time sheet in his glove box."

"A hired man, then."

"Yes. Donovan Weyer may be out of the way, but I think his employer will be here soon."

Maggie reached into her front jeans pocket and pulled out a ring of keys. She looked at them carefully before laying them on the table. "They belong to Weyer," she said in reply to the questioning gaze of the clergyman. "I thought a little counterespionage might be in order for today. If I can search his place, we might find out the name of his employer and hopefully what they are after in this house."

Maggie lifted a hot cast iron skillet from the stovetop. She moved to the table and then slid a nicely browned slice of toast onto each plate. In the center of each slice was a perfectly cooked egg. She replaced the skillet on the stovetop. "I think some sort of distraction may be the best plan. Monk, do you have one of those large stereo boxes?"

Monk looked surprised, "A boombox? Sure, there is one in my room."

"Great! And you play basketball, correct?"

"I know my way around the court. The guys and I have even learned some neat trick shots."

"Most excellent. I think we have a plan then."

"And I," added Reverend Jim, "will be praying as usual as I work on Sunday's sermon. First, however, let's thank God for this food." With all heads bowed, he continued, "Heavenly Father, thank you for your protection and provision. Bless this food to our bodies. Give us strength and insight as we investigate today. In Jesus' name. Amen."

Monk momentarily looked at the food on his plate before cutting it in half with a knife and fork. The egg yolk was not quite solid, and a small stream of golden yellow slowly flowed onto the plate. He pierced the butter-browned toast with his fork, removing a small piece that he used to sop up the yolk. A few seconds after placing it into his mouth, a smile widened across his face.

"I know, right?" said Maggie, "It's scrumptious."

The three enjoyed their breakfast of gashouse eggs and coffee. Afterward, they tidied the kitchen. Maggie looked up at the clock above the stove. It was just about nine o'clock.

"We'd better get moving." Turning to Reverend Jim, she said, "Thank you again, Jim, for the lads and your prayers. How about dinner this evening? Pizza, I think?"

"I'll come early to help with the dough," responded the kind pastor. Reverend Jim attached the leashes to Shadrach and Meshach and led them out the back door. With a quick wave, he vanished through the gate.

Chapter

VI

SUBTERFUGE ON
CHAMBERLAIN AVENUE

Maggie closed the back door and then turned to Monk. "It appears Donovan Weyer lives in that new apartment complex just inside the town limits. I noticed the address on a business card in his wallet. The same address was on some mail in his car. I remember seeing the building on my ride into town. It's the only one on Chamberlain Avenue, as far as I recall." She paused. "Here's what I need you to do. First, we'll park Magersfontein nearby, maybe a block or so away. Then, you need to set up the boombox in front of the building so all the residents can see you from their windows. Would it be possible to have a few other fellows there?"

"I think I can manage that," replied Monk.

"Good. You and your friends need to dribble and pass the basketball around in full view, with the music playing loud. You know, do some of that fancy ball-spinning and passing. That should grab the attention of the building residents and passersby. I need everyone distracted so no one sees me entering the building."

Monk nodded, "Will do." He moved into the front room and made a couple of telephone calls. Returning to the kitchen, he said, "We're all set."

After cleaning up the breakfast dishes, the two headed to the carport and then put on their gear. After Maggie turned the bike around, Monk hopped into the sidecar and settled the boombox in the footwell. She let the engine warm up for a minute or two before heading out of the driveway and down the street toward the town limit. The drive to Weyer's apartment took about ten minutes—a little longer than usual because Maggie selected backstreets.

She thought, *If the residents are as attentive as Mr. Butler, I need to remain as covert as possible.* Finally, she turned onto Chamberlain Avenue and then parked two blocks away from the apartment building. Monk pointed to a nearby phone booth.

"I told Tommy I'd call when we arrived. He and the others will be here in a snap." He removed his helmet and gloves, and then placed them inside the sidecar footwell. He walked to the glass phone booth and stepped inside. He removed a quarter from his jeans pocket and then slid it into the slot at the top of the phone. He waited for the dial tone before pushing the numbered buttons. After a few seconds, he said, "Hey, Tommy. It's Monk. Yeah, we're here. That's right. You've got the basketball? Great." He exited the phone booth and smiled. "They're just around the corner."

"Good friends, then?" asked Maggie.

"The best."

Maggie dismounted the bike and then stowed her gear. "Well, let's head that way, then."

As they rounded the street corner, Maggie noticed a modern four-story structure with little aesthetic appeal. A front entrance was in the center of the building at the ground level, and a smaller side entrance was toward the back. She could see mailboxes inside the lobby. *I'll take a quick gander over those to find Weyer's apartment number.*

Monk made his way to the front of the complex with the boombox balanced on his left shoulder. Maggie noticed three teens walking toward him from the opposite side. One of them, Tommy, she presumed, was happily bouncing a basketball. The group huddled together for a minute, and then Monk placed the boombox on the sidewalk, tuning to a popular radio station. Pop music blared from the speakers. Tommy began passing the ball between his legs and then around his back. Then he passed it to Derek, who threw the ball into the air. It landed precisely on the tip of his index finger, continuously whirling as he moved it around his back. He lifted it into the air with a toss. The ball landed on his knee where he bounced it to Monk.

"Hey, those guys are pretty good," said an older man wearing a security guard uniform. A crowd quickly surrounded the youths as they continued performing basketball tricks they learned from watching television. Some from the crowd caught the ball, performed a trick, and passed it on. Apartment windows were opened as curious residents looked out to see the spectacle. Maggie seized the moment and made her way to the side door.

Please be unlocked, she thought as she grasped the knob. It turned easily, and she opened the door. Cautiously looking inside, she noticed two people in the lobby had their backs to her, intrigued by the scene outside.

"What's all that about?" asked an older woman gruffly.

"I'm not sure," replied a middle-aged man. Maggie tiptoed to the wall of mailboxes.

Abernathy, Davis, Moore, ah-ha, there you are. Weyer, apartment 302. She continued carefully ahead to the stairs. Climbing at a steady pace, she soon reached the third floor. Apartment 302 was at the end of the empty hallway.

Maggie examined the key ring. The two marked keys went to Mr. Weyer's vehicle. She moved them to the side. *One of the remaining two keys must open the apartment door.* The smaller of the two keys looked like a mailbox key. That left only one. After slipping on her riding gloves, she inserted the key in the door lock and then turned it. Success! She quietly opened the door and then slipped inside. *I don't think I should chance checking if there's anything in the mailbox on the way out. I'll surely be noticed.*

After a quick look around, Maggie realized that Weyer lived alone. The apartment was small, unkept, and very plain. The main room was combined into a kitchen, dining room, and living room. A narrow hallway to the right led to a single bedroom with an adjoining bathroom. Maggie began her search at a small metal desk tucked into a corner of the main room. More receipts littered the desktop.

Who hired you, Mr. Weyer? She opened the single desk drawer. Inside was a museum brochure with "The Real McCoy" circled on one of the pages. Maggie glanced over the paper. *Hmm. This is from a Prohibition museum in New York. Bootleggers and speakeasies. That is very intriguing.* She tucked the brochure into her jacket pocket.

Not finding any other clues, she stepped into the small kitchen area. The countertop was cluttered with dirty dishes and take-out boxes, and the refrigerator was empty except for a single can of soda. *Definitely not well provisioned.*

The bedroom and bathroom proved equally unhelpful until she checked jacket pockets in the closet. *Success!* Her hand grasped a small piece of paper with the phone number (401) 301-3215. *A visit to the library may help us trace this number. Maybe it's Mr. Weyer's employer.* Maggie opened a black leather suitcase lying on the closet floor. She slid her gloved hands between the dividers but found nothing. Before leaving the bedroom, she felt under the pillows and mattress, but to no avail.

Moving into the bathroom, she clicked on the light and looked over the sink countertop's contents. *Toothbrush, comb, razor, shaving cream. Nothing here.* Returning to the main room, she glanced around the apartment again to ensure that things looked pretty much like she had found them. After turning off all the lights, she quietly left, locking the door behind her. The hallway was still empty. *Monk and his friends are putting on a pretty good show,* she mused.

She opened the stairwell door and then descended to the lobby. As she made her way to the side exit, she laughed to herself as she watched the small crowd tossing the basketball and dancing to the radio. Maggie went down the sidewalk, pausing at the corner to signal to the boys. Moving casually, Monk and his friends waved to the crowd, grabbed the boombox, and walked the opposite way. After about five minutes, they met Maggie where she'd parked Magersfontein. "Thank you, gentlemen. I can't tell you how much I appreciate your help!"

"Anything for Miss Mary," said a tall, blond lad. "I'm Tommy, by the way, and this is Larry and Derek."

"It is a pleasure to meet you."

"That's about the most exciting thing we've done in a while!" said Derek.

"Yeah, a lot more fun than catching insects for your collection," teased Larry.

"Reading between the lines," said Tommy, "you were looking for some clues in one of the apartments?"

"Yes," Maggie said hesitantly. She recounted the previous night's events while the young men listened intently.

"That sounds even more exciting than today," said Derek. Wow! Whoever thought this kind of stuff could happen in Kevan's Cove."

With a serious tone, Tommy said, "So the man you captured last night is the same one who attacked Miss Mary?"

"Yes, but we don't think he's acting alone. That's why I needed to look over his apartment." Maggie paused. "And I did find some leads."

"Anything we can help with?" asked Larry.

"A little research at the library, where Monk and I are headed next, but thank you. I'm sure I'll need your help very soon. As a way of saying thanks, how about pizza tonight at Mary's house? Around six-thirty?" All three boys nodded their heads eagerly. "Well, until then, gentlemen." At this, Maggie started the bike, and Monk sat in the sidecar. With a roar of the engine, they were off toward the library.

Chapter

VII

THE REAL MCCOY

The Kevan's Cove public library was located two blocks from the courthouse. It was an older building designed with a large glass block entrance and a wide, spiral staircase leading to the upper level. While not an extensive library, it was by no means lacking in content.

Upon entering the building, Maggie and Monk approached the main desk. Maggie quietly asked the librarian, "Telephone directories, please?" The librarian pointed to her left. Maggie nodded thanks and then she and Monk headed in the indicated direction. On a bookshelf against an outer wall were numerous phone directories. She removed the paper with the phone number from her pocket. In a whispered voice, she said, "Let's see, area code 401. That population would be somewhat sizeable."

Monk, looking confused, quietly asked, "What does the number have to do with the population?" Maggie smiled.

"You remember rotary phones, right?" Monk nodded.

"Mrs. Weaver down the street still has one."

"Well, when direct dialing was becoming a thing, area codes were assigned by population, with the most populous cities having the numbered area codes that were quicker to dial on the rotary dial."

"Direct-dialing?"

"Dial the entire number yourself, versus having a switchboard operator connect your phone to the long-distance area. You know, like in the old movies when they turned a crank on the phone to signal the operator." Monk's face showed an *aha* look and Maggie continued, "Since the phone company required people to dial the complete number, areas with more phone lines were given numbers closer to the start of the rotary dial. Therefore, if we have a 401 area code, it should be a moderately populated area." She paused. "On the other hand, it could be an entire state." She randomly pulled a phonebook from the shelf and opened it to the front. "Here we go, an area code map. 401 is—"

Rhode Island," completed Monk. He scanned the shelf and quickly retrieved a Rhode Island directory.

"Now," Maggie continued, "some directories have listings by names only while others include an additional listing by number. I'm praying that this one has both."

Monk quickly fanned through the first part of the directory, where names were listed alphabetically. Sure enough, a section at the back was ordered by phone numbers, with the corresponding name to the right. The two scanned page after page until finally, they found (401) 301-3215. Following the number was the name Maxwell McCoy. Maggie pulled the brochure from her jacket pocket and showed it to Monk.

"The Real McCoy. This must be the connection." Removing a pen from the same pocket, Maggie wrote down the address from the phone book. "While here, let's see what the library has on our rum runner from the brochure." Monk replaced the phonebook, and then the two quietly moved to the card catalog.

The catalog comprised seven wooden cabinets, each with twelve drawers. The front of each drawer displayed a label showing a range of partial words ordered alphabetically. Maggie slowly scanned the labels until she came to the section beginning with the letter R. She then narrowed her search to the drawer with the range *rul* to *rum*. She opened the drawer and then flipped through the cards until she came to *rum runner*.

"Here's a book titled *The Real McCoy* by Frederic F. Van de Water. Let's get this from the stacks and check it out." Monk moved to the desk beside the card catalog and picked up a piece of scrap paper and a stubby pencil. Returning to Maggie, he glanced at the card and wrote down the book's call number. The two looked up at a sign on a column beside the catalog to determine if the book was in the upstairs stacks or the main level. Monk was the first to point up with his index finger.

Quietly exiting the main level, they went to the vestibule and up the spiral staircase to the upper level. Maggie and Monk walked slowly in front of the shelves, reading each row's sign until they found the one containing the book's call number range. Midway through the aisle, Monk suddenly reached out and removed the book.

"Excellent work, Monk," Maggie whispered, and the two retraced their steps to the main desk on the first level. Monk handed the book and his library card to the librarian. She removed, stamped, and filed the book card and then handed the book and library card back to Monk.

"It is due in two weeks," she said.

Monk smiled and nodded, saying a soft, "Thank you."

Back outside in the parking lot, Maggie started Magersfontein while Monk tucked the library book safely in the sidecar compartment. With helmets on, the two rode through town to the police station. Maggie pulled into a parallel parking spot in front of the building.

"Wait here for me, okay?" she said after shutting off the engine. "I'll only be a moment." She pulled Weyers' keyring from her leather jacket pocket and flashed Monk a Cheshire cat smile. True to her word, Maggie returned just a few minutes later. "I left them with the desk sergeant. Now, let's get home and start dinner. Reverend Jim will be over soon, and I have a lot of studying to do." Taking a brief pause, she continued, "How about pie for dessert?" Monk nodded hungrily. "Where is the best bakery in town, then?"

"Shoofly Pies is on the way home. Mrs. Williams' pies can't be beat." Monk stopped and then quickly added, "But don't tell Miss Mary I said that."

"My lips are sealed," smiled Maggie.

"It's on the right, about a block before Maple Street."

Magers purred along the quaint main street. Kevan's Cove, though small, was not without its charm. Wrought iron fences outlined the well-manicured lawns of attractive bungalows and Cape Cod houses. A few majestic manors were built by the town's elite, but most of the architecture was sensible and practical. Stopping to observe the red light of the town's only traffic signal, Maggie turned right and then pulled into the parking lot of a small bakery. The air was filled with the aroma of freshly baked bread.

"Mmm," said Maggie as she removed her helmet and breathed deeply. Monk smiled and did the same. They stowed their gear and when they opened the bakery door, a small bell at the top of the door jingled.

"Hello, Monk," said a pleasant older woman.

"Hi, Mrs. Williams." Turning to Maggie, he continued, "This is Maggie North, a friend of Miss Mary." The two women shook hands.

"What can I do you for, then?"

"Two pies, please. Maybe make one a rhubarb pie?" asked Maggie.

"I'll check on the rhubarb. What about the second one?"

"I'll leave that up to you." After disappearing through a doorway behind the counter, the woman quickly returned.

"Last rhubarb and," winking at Monk, she continued, "my chocolate meringue pie, just out of the oven. I believe that's one of your favorites." Monk nodded eagerly. "Let me get these boxed and bagged for y'all."

"Thank you." Maggie continued, "Have you lived in Kevan's Cove long?"

"All my life."

"What can you tell me about Miss Mary's house?" Mrs. Williams looked slightly intrigued by the question.

"Old Captain Smith's place? Let me see. He had that built when he retired. Quite a character, Captain Smith. He stopped in every morning for coffee and cinnamon rolls. Oh, the stories that man could tell! He was always going on about his rum running days." She paused, "You know, he once told me he was a millionaire. Ha! And him wearing those ragged clothes and a worn-out hat. What an imagination he had. Now, let me see. He was from Rhode Island originally.

Inherited some property there, I believe." Mrs. Williams laughed, "He called it his seaside shack. He would go back home every spring to check on his other house and visit with old shipmates. Sadly, he died there. Unusual circumstances, I remember."

"Unusual?" queried Maggie, probing for more information.

Mrs. Williams continued, "Yes, it looked like a heart attack, but there were some questions. You see, he didn't have a history of heart problems. He was older, though, so the authorities ruled it death by natural causes. Since there was no will and no relatives came forward, the state auctioned off the house here in Kevan's Cove. I don't know what happened to the other one in Rhode Island."

She handed Monk a large paper bag across the counter and said, "Here you go." Maggie smiled and exchanged payment for the pies.

"Thank you," said Maggie, "for the pies and the information." Mrs. Williams smiled and waved as the two exited, the bell ringing as the door closed behind them.

Back at the bike, she continued, "That's interesting. We have Captain Smith–I'm assuming that captain was an earned title–and McCoy, the rum runner. There appears to be a nautical connection in all of this."

"If there is, it may be in the library book?"

"Yes, Monk, I think so. God, in his goodness, has been guiding us. Now I'm praying for the wisdom to decipher the information he has shown us."

Motioning to the bike, Maggie continued, "Shall we?" Once suited up and securely seated, the two were off toward Maple Street.

Chapter

VIII

THE MAGDALA LEAGUE EXPLAINED

Maggie shut off the engine and then looked at her wristwatch. "Missed lunch again." She walked to the back door, opening it as Monk carefully carried the pies inside. Maggie followed him to the kitchen. He made another trip to bring in the boombox.

"Reverend Jim and I were thinking we would have a homemade pizza party. You know, everyone making a personal pie with their toppings of choice. Does that sound okay?"

Monk smiled. "Sounds terrific! I sure am hungry!"

"How are you at chopping vegetables?"

"I hold my own."

"Excellent. Reverend Jim will be along shortly. He always insists on making the dough, so that means we're stuck preparing the toppings." She comically frowned at Monk. Just then, there was a quick rap on the screen door.

"Come on in, Reverend. We're just getting started." The clergyman entered through the door carrying a large paper grocery bag. He was followed by Shadrach and Meshach, who obediently sat down. After placing the bag on the counter, he knelt and then unhooked their leashes.

Peeking into the bag, Maggie smiled. "You didn't have to bring the supplies."

"I know, but I've wanted to try out this flour. It's specifically ground for pizza dough. I think it will make the best pizza crust yet."

Turning to Monk, Maggie said, "I'll bet you didn't know that Reverend Jim is a pizza connoisseur."

Monk looked a bit surprised. "I'm beginning to realize that there is much more to the people in my life than I first thought."

"That, my boy, is true of everyone," said Reverend Jim. "All of us have a story to live out here on this earth. God wrote it and set it into motion even before we were born. '[Y]our eyes saw my unformed body. All the days ordained for me were written in your book before one of them came to be.' (Psalm 139:16). God lets us cross paths and share stories with other people. Sometimes, we learn something. Sometimes, we share something. Sometimes, we do both."

Monk turned to Maggie. "Now is as good a time as any to tell me about my mother."

Maggie and Reverend Jim glanced at each other. "Alright, I will," she said as she reached into the cabinet and handed Reverend Jim some mixing bowls.

Jim set them on the table and then began unpacking the supplies from the bag. Smiling, he said, "I'm a little particular about what I put on my pizza, so I brought the ingredients I like."

"I think I noticed Mary's canned sauce in the pantry," said Maggie. "And there's some fresh mozzarella in the refrigerator. I don't think she'll mind if we use it."

Monk opened the refrigerator door and then placed the packaged mozzarella balls on the table, along with a wedge of Parmesan cheese. "And," he said, "she always keeps a pepperoni stick for me."

"Well," said Maggie, "let's prepare the toppings while I tell you about your mother. She was a Magdala, as you know." Monk looked up from chopping, and Maggie continued, "She came to the League a couple of years before I did and was well ahead of me in training. Maddie was in the missions program. She was called to assist missionaries in remote countries. God gave your mother a pretty clear vision of her story. This was in sharp contrast to me. I'm one of the ones whose steps God illuminates only as I need to take them," she laughed.

"Your mother completed her training ahead of schedule and was sent to Brazil to work alongside some missionaries. That was where she met your father. It was clear that God meant for them to be together. While Maddie had envisioned a lifetime of single service in the Magdala League, her love for your father was an unexpected gift from God. With much prayer, she realized that God's story for her was richer and more profound than she could imagine. So, she embraced the change and married Ben. You came along about a year later."

"I don't remember much about my parents," said Monk. He had stopped chopping now, and tears were forming in his eyes.

"Well, you were very young when they were killed. Your mother, perceiving that things were becoming hostile where they were posted, sent word to the League to get you to safety."

Turning to the young man and touching his shoulder, Maggie continued, "You see, Monk, I was the one who got you out of Brazil. The native tribe killed your parents within days." Teardrops streamed down Monk's face.

Maggie paused to wipe her own eyes and then continued, "I know, but God has a way of bringing things full circle. Once again, our stories are joined in a great adventure. Let's make it count. Okay?"

Monk nodded and wiped his tears on the sleeve of his shirt. "I miss them."

"I do, too. I keep thinking of 2 Corinthians 5:6-9. 'Therefore we are always confident and know that as long as we are at home in the body we are away from the Lord. We live by faith, not by sight. We are confident, I say, and would prefer to be away from the body and at home with the Lord. So we make it our goal to please him, whether we are at home in the body or away from it.' Your parents are present with the Lord. We, who are still here, must continue God's work."

With a slight thump, Reverend Jim plopped the pizza dough into a mixing bowl and covered it with a towel. "Well, the dough has to rise for about an hour. Monk, how about you and I take the lads for a stroll?"

This brought some light into the young man's face as he moved to the sink to wash his hands. After drying them on a towel, he reached for the leashes and called to the dogs.

"And I," said Maggie, "will be here chopping toppings and grating cheese." The walking party exited through the back door, down the driveway, and onto the sidewalk.

"So, what's Maggie's story?" asked Monk.

"Maggie North," began Reverend Jim. "That's quite a tale, and I only know some of it." He paused, "I understand she came from a somewhat affluent background. Relations with her family were strained. You see, she struggled quite a bit to meet their expectations. How should I put this? Maggie is a bit of a wild one."

Seeing the look of surprise on Monk's face, the old clergyman quickly qualified the statement. "Oh, no, not in the sense of being immoral or rebellious. It's just that God gave her a spirit that this world can't seem to tame. She's restless, always seeking adventure, pursuing truth. She's not satisfied with things down here, this earthly existence, I mean. Which, I think, is how we all should be in some respect or another. She was a bit of a

71

handful at the Magdala League academy, not fitting into the traditional training courses. Ultimately, they created a new branch of the organization for Maggie and others like her. Of course, her family disapproved of her joining the league. They had her life all planned out. All disapproved except for an eccentric, old aunt. She left her entire estate to Maggie, which funded the new program. God worked it all out. And Maggie, well, she does some of his more dangerous work."

"I had no idea," said Monk, "but I'm grateful to God for her, not only for what she did in the past but also for coming here to help Miss Mary and me."

"She thrives on little puzzles like this, and if I'm honest, so do I."

"What is the connection between Maggie and Miss Mary?" asked Monk. "I mean, besides them both being in the League."

"Ah, yes, well, as I said, Maggie had a little trouble fitting into the training at the academy. Mary, seeing tremendous potential, mentored her and was instrumental in Maggie's training. I understand she designed the Special Operations Section—SOS for short—herself. Mary has some military training, you know." Monk's face looked surprised.

Reverend Jim continued, "Maggie has never forgotten Mary's kindness. She's loyal to her through and through. So now you can understand why she came here so quickly." Monk nodded and Jim said, "It's a lot for you to process, my lad—your parents, Miss Mary and Maggie. Just know, God has all of this well in hand."

"I know," Monk said. He paused and added, "Thank you. It's just so bittersweet. I had no idea that Maggie—." His voice sounded broken.

"She's always been looking out for you. In fact, she was the one who arranged for Mary to have custody of you when your aunt passed away."

"It's only that a week ago, I had no clue about the Magdala League, and now," he paused, his eyes tearing up, "well, you're right. It is a lot to process."

Reverend Jim gave him a reassuring squeeze on the shoulder. "Just remember that our lives here are strange, wonderful, and bittersweet, but they are best lived with complete surrender to God's will."

Chapter

Pizza, Pie, and Providence

By the time the walking party returned, Maggie had finished preparing the toppings and had set three jars of Mary's tomato sauce on the countertop. "Monk's friends will be here in about twenty minutes," she said. I guess it's time to get the oven heated, and the pizza pans out."

Smiling at Monk, she added, "Have you ever seen Reverend Jim toss pizza dough?" Monk, wide-eyed, shook his head from side to side.

Reverend Jim replied, "It is a hidden talent of mine."

"Can you teach me?" asked the young man eagerly. Reverend Jim smiled.

"Certainly. Let's get washed up and have a go." The two took turns washing and drying their hands at the kitchen sink. Reverend Jim moved the flour sack from the countertop to the table. He uncovered the bowl of pizza dough, which had risen nicely and was now more than double in size. Reaching into the open flour sack, he grabbed a small handful and then sprinkled it on a section of the table. Next, he pinched off some dough and lightly coated it with flour.

"First, we remove air bubbles from the dough by flattening it." Monk first watched and then imitated Reverend Jim's technique, sprinkling flour on the dough to prevent it from sticking to his fingers or the table.

"There you go! Next, with both hands, stretch the dough in opposite directions. That's right. Now turn it a half-turn and do the same thing again."

After watching Monk for a few seconds, Reverend Jim continued, "Now take it off the table and hold it with the back of your knuckles." He glanced at Monk's hands. "Yes, that's right. Remember, it's important to keep turning the dough to let gravity work and stretch it out." Starting awkwardly at first, Monk soon began to get the hang of it.

"Nice work! Now for the exciting part. To toss it, keep it on your knuckles and then lift with your fingertips to fling it into the air, like this." With a quick motion, Reverend Jim took the dough, tossed it into the air, and gracefully caught it with the backs of his knuckles. "Toss it about three to four times until it looks like this."

After the fourth toss, Reverend Jim carefully slid the dough onto the floured table. It was even throughout and just thick enough to hold the sauce, toppings, and cheese. "Alright, Monk, give it a go."

Monk's first toss was a little awkward. "That's alright, keep at it. Don't think about dropping it. Just give it a good toss." The second toss was a little higher and more even. "I think you're getting the hang of it!"

It was about this time that the front doorbell rang. "I'll get it," said Maggie. Opening the door, she exclaimed, "Y'all are just in time. Monk's tossing pizza dough with Reverend Jim!"

Wide-eyed, Tommy, Larry, and Derek rushed to the kitchen.

"Come on," smiled Monk, "grab some dough. It's a blast!" With that, Reverend Jim repeated his instructions on the art of pizza tossing. Before long, the table was full of dough circles, some round and even, others less so.

"Time to build the pizzas," directed Reverend Jim. He demonstrated by rubbing a little olive oil on the pizza dough, followed by a spoonful of sauce and some oregano. He then added his toppings of choice. "Now for the cheese." The clergyman pinched off pieces of mozzarella and spread them over the pie. Grabbing a small grater, he topped it off with a generous coating of Parmesan cheese. Then, with the help of a pizza peel, he slid the completed pie onto a large cookie sheet. "And into the oven it goes!"

Eagerly, each young man followed suit, customizing their pizza to suit their taste.

As pizzas rotated in and out of the oven, Reverend Jim said, "Let's give God thanks for this food." The room quickly fell silent. All eyes were closed, and heads bowed. "Our great and good Father, thank you for providing for our daily needs. Thank you for this food and fellowship. We pray for Mary. Please heal her wounds and increase her strength. Protect us all and continue to guide us. Amen."

Multiple *amens* sounded around the room, and the young men resumed their buzz of conversation.

"It's time for our favorite TV show," said Monk. Turning to Maggie, he asked, "Would it be alright if we ate in the front room?"

"Absolutely, but no messes. We need to keep things neat and tidy." A chorus of "Yes, ma'am" followed.

After the kitchen had emptied of hungry teenagers, Reverend Jim turned to Maggie. "What pieces of the puzzle do we have so far?"

"Well, there aren't any flies on you, are there?" said Maggie with a laugh. She momentarily left the room and then returned with the books and papers she and Monk had collected. "You're right. I'm certain there's something valuable in this house, and Weyer was hired to find it. McCoy fits into it somewhere, but how?"

"McCoy?" Reverend Jim asked as he picked up the library book and flipped through the pages, primarily looking at the photos. Maggie did the same with Erasmus Beauregard's book on the houses of Kevan's Cove.

"We traced a phone number I found at Weyer's apartment using the phone directories at the library. The number is registered to a Maxwell McCoy of

Rhode Island." She suddenly stopped. "Wait a minute. Mrs. Williams said that Captain Smith was originally from Rhode Island. He owned a seaside cottage there."

"And 'The Real McCoy?'" asked Jim as he held up the museum pamphlet tucked inside the library book.

"I found that at Weyers's apartment." She paused, pointing to the page in front of her. "Here's Captain Smith's house."

Reverend Jim glanced over at Maggie's open book. On one of the pages was a photo of a white-haired man with a full beard smoking a pipe in front of a fireplace.

"Wait a minute," he said. "I just saw him!" He flipped a few pages back in the library book and pointed to a picture of the same man, sans beard, standing beside William McCoy on one of the rum runner's ships.

Maggie and Reverend Jim looked at each other in astonishment, then said in unison, "The Real McCoy!" At this juncture, Tommy entered the kitchen in search of more pizza.

Glancing at the book in Maggie's hand, he said, "Hey, that's the model ship from the hobby shop."

"What ship?" asked Reverend Jim.

"The one on the mantel in that photo. It's a beauty!" Maggie and Reverend Jim looked at each other and then at the photo, focusing on the model ship in the background.

"You know the hobby shop owner pretty well?" asked Maggie.

"Mr. Comer, sure! I'm into model railroading, and his shop has a great selection of parts."

"Would it be possible for you to meet Monk and me at the hobby shop tomorrow, Tommy?" asked Maggie.

"Sure thing! I need to pick up more track anyway."

"About ten o'clock, then?"

"You got it." As Tommy rejoined the others in the living room, Maggie turned to Reverend Jim.

"You know your nautical flags, right?"

"Once a Navy man, always a Navy man!"

"Well, take a look at this." She held the book closer to him and pointed to the flags on the ship.

"Kilo, 9, Echo. Let's see, that translates to 'I wish to communicate, nine, altering course to starboard.'" He paused a moment. "There's more to the message, but the rest of the flags are out of the picture."

"Is it a code?"

"More like directions, I think, but directions to where and to what? Communicate means a message. The number nine could be steps or feet. Starboard means to turn right. Maybe it's a safe combination?" Lost in thought, he continued. "I'll be at the hobby shop tomorrow as well."

Maggie looked upward and prayed, "Jesus, thank you for clearing our minds and giving us this revelation." Reverend Jim closed the books and moved them to the side of the table.

"And now for some pie."

Larry, as if on cue, quickly entered the room. "Did someone say pie?"

"Chocolate or rhubarb?" asked Maggie.

Chapter

A Tall Ship with a Tall Tale

Maggie awoke early, as usual, except she was a little less rested this morning. Her mind had been busy all night pondering the meaning of the flags and the connection between McCoy and Captain Smith. It was useless until they had the entire message, but her mind simply wouldn't shut down. After cleaning up and changing from her pajamas into black denim overalls and a white t-shirt, she retrieved the familiar percolator and then began making coffee.

Looking in a side cabinet, she noticed Mary had preserved last season's pick from the sour cherry tree in the backyard. *Yes, I think biscuits for breakfast,* she said to herself as she washed her hands in the kitchen sink.

While the coffee bubbled on the stovetop, Maggie gathered the supplies and then set them on the counter. Her thoughts were far away as she mixed ingredients.

The nautical code in the flags is directions to something, but what? She mentally reviewed the book pages she read the night before. *Captain Smith worked for William McCoy during Prohibition. He made trips from Canada to the East Coast, where he delivered rum and other spirits. If I remember correctly, the ship would have remained in international waters until the cargo was unloaded. What if he came across something valuable on one of his trips? But which shore, Canada or the US?*

Maggie remembered her conversation with Pat at the Kevan's Cove Historical Society. *That's right, the East Coast was a favorite hideout of pirates. They even came to Kevan's Cove. Could Captain Smith have found some valuable relics from a pirate shipwreck?*

Maggie placed the biscuit dough on the counter. As she lightly kneaded it, her mind turned to Max McCoy. *How does McCoy fit into all of this? Mrs. Williams said Captain Smith died in Rhode Island while visiting some old shipmates. What if Max McCoy is related to one of those old shipmates, William McCoy, for instance? A cousin or nephew, maybe? I know from the book that William McCoy moved to Florida after his rum running days. However, Max McCoy lives in Rhode Island. He may have had something to do with the captain's death!*

She stopped herself. *Hold on, Margaret India North, don't get too carried away. You can't prove that. It's just conjecture at this point. However, McCoy may be looking for something the captain found on one of his voyages and hired Donovan to find it. What if Captain Smith was indeed a millionaire like he told Mrs. Williams? Money, or greed, I should say, is a definite motive.*

Using a Mason jar, Maggie cut out twelve circles of dough. She opened a bottom cabinet near the oven. Reaching inside, she pulled out a cookie sheet. Next, she drizzled cooking oil on it and smoothed it with her hand. Then, she carefully placed the biscuits on the sheet. After sliding it into the oven, she washed up at the kitchen sink.

"I think I need some coffee," she said with exasperation. She was about to pour a cup when a sleepy-eyed Monk entered the kitchen.

"Mmm. What smells so good?"

"Coffee and biscuits. The biscuits will be ready in just a few minutes. Until then, how about some coffee?"

The young man smiled and sat down at the kitchen table. Maggie poured him a steaming cup and then sat in a nearby chair. "So, what's this about going to the hobby shop today?"

Maggie reached for the books she and Reverend Jim had left on the table the evening before. She first opened the library book on William McCoy, pointing to the photo of two men on the deck of a sailing vessel. Next, in the local book on prominent houses, she pointed to the section showing Captain Smith's house. Monk looked repeatedly at the two books. "Hey. It's the same man. A little older and with a beard, but it's the same guy!"

"Look closely at the background in this picture," said Maggie.

"Isn't that the model ship from the hobby shop?"

"Exactly! And what do you know about nautical flags?"

"A little. Each stands for a letter or number. The letter flags also have an additional meaning."

"And by God's providence," said Maggie, "Reverend Jim is a retired Navy chaplain. Last evening, he determined that there was a message in the flags."

"Oh, now I understand!" exclaimed Monk. "But not all the flags are in the picture."

"Correct," said Maggie. "Ergo, the visit to the hobby shop this morning. Tommy said that Mr. Comer has the model ship on display in his store."

She turned to the oven, opened the door, and then removed the sheet of golden brown biscuits. After sliding them onto a plate, she placed them on the table with two small plates, two dinner knives, a stick of butter, and Mary's sour cherry preserves.

"Father, thank you for caring for us and for this delicious food. Bless our quest today. Protect us and enlighten our minds. We love you, and thank you. Amen."

"Amen," repeated Monk. He grabbed a hot biscuit and carefully split it in half, laying the fluffy, steaming halves on his plate. After adding healthy portions of butter and preserves, he reassembled the biscuit and happily took a bite. Maggie did the same.

"I was just thinking," said Maggie, "about what Mrs. Williams told us. She said Captain Smith died suspiciously while staying at his property in Rhode Island. McCoy lives in Rhode Island."

"You think McCoy had something to do with Captain Smith's death?"

"I'm not sure, but it would make sense if he knew the captain had some valuable property. You know, the captain could have come across some relics from a shipwreck on one of his voyages."

Monk continued, "And McCoy hasn't found it so far."

"Exactly. He couldn't locate it in the house in Rhode Island, but somehow found out about the captain's house here in Kevan's Cove. That's why Weyer was here. It also means he's intent on getting it, no matter what. The quicker we can solve this mystery, the better."

After drinking more coffee, she continued, "How about driving Magersfontein to the hobby shop?" The young man eagerly nodded his head up and down since his mouth was full of biscuits, butter, and preserves. "Take it slow at first. While it is a bike, the sidecar makes it quite different to steer."

"I understand," he said after washing down his mouthful with a sip of coffee. "And thank you." They spent the rest of the breakfast in contented silence, savoring the fare. After washing the dishes, they headed outside to the driveway.

"Let him warm up a bit first," said Maggie, handing Monk the key. Monk stood in front of the motorcycle and squeezed the clutch with his right hand. While pushing the bike, he turned the handlebars so it rolled into the turnaround in the driveway, just as he had watched Maggie do before. He then sat astride the bike and started the engine. The two put on their helmets and gloves, and then Maggie climbed into the sidecar.

After a minute, Monk eased the bike down the driveway and then turned right onto the road. Maggie raised a thumbs-up in approval.

They continued slowly down the road, with Monk gradually picking up a little speed as he got the hang of steering Magersfontein. In due time, they arrived at the hobby shop. Monk glided into an open parking spot and then shut off the engine.

"Good job, Monk," said Maggie. Monk smiled with a newfound sense of accomplishment. They removed their helmets and, after stowing them, alighted from the bike. The pair walked to the storefront and opened the door of Harry's Hobby Shop.

Tommy, Larry, and Derek were already inside, along with Reverend Jim, who was carefully eyeing a model ship in the corner of the shop. Maggie made her way to him and softly asked, "Well?"

"It's the same one, alright, but I think there is more to it than just the flags."

"Well, then, let's see if we can buy it," Maggie said. She went to the counter in the center of the store and began conversing with Mr. Comer, the Harry in the hobby shop's name. "Hi, I'm Maggie North, a friend of Mary Wright."

"Oh, poor Mary," the man said. "How is she?"

"A little better, but still weak."

"Our quiet community was so shocked when we heard what happened to her. Please tell her that I'm praying for her."

"I will, and thank you," replied Maggie. "Is the model ship in the corner for sale?"

"Old Captain Smith's ship? I bought it at the estate sale with the idea of displaying it in the shop, but if it's for Mary, then the answer is affirmative. It belongs in that house anyway."

Maggie and Mr. Comer quickly agreed on the price, and the sale was completed. Upon ascertaining that the ship had been purchased, Reverend Jim gingerly carried it to the counter.

"Thank you ever so much," Maggie said to Mr. Comer. "I know Miss Mary will be surprised to see this when she gets home."

"You are very welcome." He took the ship from Reverend Jim and carefully wrapped it in brown paper and tape. When he finished, he handed it back.

Maggie moved toward the group of young friends, who were helping Tommy select pieces for his model railroad. "Hey, Monk. Reverend Jim and I are going to take our package home. I assume you want to stay a little longer?"

Monk smiled and nodded.

"No problem, we'll see you for lunch then. That includes all of y'all."

"Yes, ma'am!" eagerly replied all four in unison.

Chapter

#

The Flags' Message

Maggie and Reverend Jim exited the shop and donned their helmets. Reverend Jim carefully situated himself in the sidecar before Maggie handed him the neatly wrapped model ship. She then climbed on Magersfontein.

Looking in the rearview mirror, she noticed an older silver-colored European luxury car parked across the street. *Hmm. I haven't seen that car before in Kevan's Cove. Rhode Island tags, too.* Turning on the engine, she eased onto the street and watched the car from the mirrors. The vehicle left its parking space and entered the roadway. While it maintained a slight distance, it was clear to Maggie that it was following them.

The windows were tinted, thus obscuring the driver's face. However, Maggie was confident it was the mysterious Mr. McCoy. *Given this*, she told herself, *the ship might best be kept at the parsonage for now.*

Maggie turned a street earlier than planned and parked in front of the church. Reverend Jim, discerning something was up, played along as he and Maggie made their way up the sidewalk. The silver car slowly coasted by as Reverend Jim opened the manse door.

"You saw something?" queried Reverend Jim after closing the door.

"That silver car. It was at the Hobby Shop when we left and followed us here. I think it's Max McCoy."

"If that's so, then it means more danger," said Reverend Jim.

"Yes, I'm afraid so. We need God's guidance to wrap this matter up quickly."

"Alright then, let's start by having a look at this ship," said Reverend Jim. "Maybe someplace out of street view?"

"I think that would be wise."

"My study is just the place." He led the way through a connecting hallway between the manse and the church. Once in the church, Reverend Jim opened a door and clicked on a light, revealing a small room encircled with bookshelves. The one window in the room faced away from the street.

"Perfect," said Maggie. After carefully placing the model ship on the table, Reverend Jim unwrapped it.

"Now, let's see what we have. Kilo, 9, Echo, 5, India, 1. That works out to a communication, the number nine, alter course to starboard, the number five, alter course to port, and the number one." He paused before continuing, "It can't be a safe combination since there are only two changes in direction. It must be directions to something."

"I agree," said Maggie, "something that is in Mary's house, but where is the starting point for the 9, starboard, 5, and so on?"

"I think the answer to that is in the photo of Captain Smith. If you remember, the ship is on the mantel in the front room."

"Of course!" exclaimed Maggie. "We start from the mantel!"

"There's something else," Reverend Jim continued. This model has an unusual feature. Do you see this small groove around the center mast?"

"Yes," answered Maggie.

"Well," he continued, "I believe it's hollow." He carefully removed a corner of sail fastened to the mast, then twisted the top piece of wood back and forth while pulling it upward. Slowly, the top of the mast came off.

Looking inside, Reverend Jim exclaimed, "Aha, I was right! There's something here!" He reached into his desk drawer and retrieved a thin, pointed letter opener that resembled a miniature sword. Inserting it into the hollow mast, he lifted out a piece of cotton string. Carefully grasping the string, he pulled it out of its hiding place.

"A key!" they chorused together.

"I think I'll put these in a safe place. With McCoy lurking around, we need to be cautious. Help me with this rug, Maggie."

Maggie moved behind the desk and began to lift the soft carpet that cushioned the heavy desk from the tiled floor beneath it. It was a large oriental rug that stretched from wall to wall with just enough space for the fringed edge to lay neatly against the base molding. As Maggie rolled up one end of the rug, she noticed a slight variation in the tile pattern.

"A floor safe! Aren't you full of surprises, Reverend Jim?"

"I can't let you have all the fun you know." Reverend Jim opened the desk drawer and removed a small paper clip with one end straightened out to form a 90-degree angle with the curved part. Slipping the clip between and under the floor tile, he pulled up gently to reveal a metal compartment just beneath the tile. Then he reached into his pocket and removed a key ring. After shuffling through a few keys, he pushed the correct one into the lock and then turned it to open the door.

"It might be a tight fit," he said as he eyed the dimensions of the open cavity. However, with skilled precision, the clergyman maneuvered the model ship carefully into the safe.

"Well, that was God's providence. It just fits." He replaced the safe cover and locked it. "Return that tile to its place and roll out the rug again." He removed the key from his ring and said, "For extra security, I think I'll keep this key in another hiding place." He moved to a side book cabinet and pulled out a crematory urn being used as a bookend. Lifting the top, he pushed the key into the contents.

With concern, Maggie asked, "Who's in there?"

"No one," laughed the clergyman. "Just flour and charcoal. I find that it acts as a deterrent, even to the nosiest of parishioners." Maggie laughed and then smiled admiringly at his cleverness.

He said, "And I'll be over for lunch. We must find a way to trap McCoy before he injures one of us again."

Maggie nodded. "I'll see you in a few, then?"

"Yes. I'll bring the fixings."

Maggie left the church through the front door. She watched the silver car parked across the street from the corner of her eye. After putting on her riding gear, she coasted onto the road. The car did the same. As before, it maintained a slight distance from Magersfontein. *Thank you, Father, that McCoy is following me. That means he doesn't suspect the model ship to be important.*

Maggie pulled into the driveway and parked Magers under the carport. She casually walked to the backdoor to give the impression she wasn't aware of McCoy's presence. Once inside, she locked the door and then rushed up the stairs to the front-facing bedroom. Kneeling on the floor, she peeked through the lace curtains to the street below.

The driver's side door of the car opened, and a man who looked to be in his mid-fifties stepped out. He lit a cigarette and then puffed on it while propped against the car. *What a nasty habit*, Maggie thought.

The man was of average height with shaggy grey-brown hair and an ill-trimmed mustache. He was wearing a well-worn leather jacket with faded blue jeans. After finishing the cigarette, McCoy threw it to the ground and then shut the car door. He walked down the sidewalk a few feet before crossing the street.

Maggie stood up to the side of the window to keep the man in view. He slowly walked by the front of the house, studying it as he passed, utterly unaware that he was being observed from the upper level. When he reached the driveway entrance, he suddenly stopped.

Maggie, making use of the abrupt pause, moved to the other side window for a better view. *I think I'm beginning to see your scheme, Mr. McCoy. Planning on sneaking in through the cellar entrance, are we?*

The man suddenly lifted his head toward the back hedge and then resumed walking down the sidewalk, but at a much quicker pace.

In the distance, Maggie heard the excited whines of the lads. *Right on time, Reverend Jim!* She went downstairs to the backdoor and then opened it just as Shadrach and Meshach mounted the steps. She motioned for Revered Jim to enter quickly, then closed and locked the door.

"Max McCoy was just here!"

"What?"

"Yes. He followed me home. He seems overly interested in the cellar door."

"Oh, he is, is he? Well, that gives us a head start."

"Yes, it does, but it will have to be nearly foolproof. I don't want Monk or his friends hurt."

"I know you worry about him, Maggie, but he can take care of himself. I think we need to involve those youngsters in the plan. More ears, eyes, and hands, you know."

With hesitation, Maggie said, "Oh, very well. You're right, as usual." Looking at the clock, she continued, "We'd better get started on lunch, or we'll soon have four hungry teenagers on our hands and no food."

Reverend Jim laughed. "Alright. Let me put the lads out back."

Chapter

Liaison Over Lasagna

True to his word, Reverend Jim had brought all the ingredients for lunch. "So, what are we eating?" asked Maggie.

"Lasagna with garlic bread."

"Mmm, one of my favorites! Let's get cookin', shall we?" She opened a cabinet door and found two saucepans, a skillet, and a large baking dish. Then, she filled one of the saucepans with water before setting it to boil on the stovetop. She would heat the tomato sauce in the other saucepan, and meanwhile chopped mushrooms and onions into the skillet.

"Now to the tomato sauce," began Reverend Jim, "we'll add some olive oil, oregano, salt, and pepper. Put the chopped garlic cloves and some oregano with the mushrooms and onions." The heat of the pan intensified the already pleasing aroma. "And I brought some of my sourdough bread. It's a day old, which means it's perfect for garlic bread."

"Wow!" replied Maggie. "The smell of the oregano is wonderful." Once the water began to boil, Reverend Jim added the ribbon-like lasagna noodles.

"When these finish cooking, we'll assemble the lasagna." Sitting at the table, he continued, "Now, what are we going to do about this McCoy fellow?"

"Yes, there are plenty of unknowns," said Maggie as she sat opposite him.

"Such as how much does he know?" replied Reverend Jim.

"I don't think he knows about the code in the ship's flags. When I left you at the church, I noticed he was reading a newspaper in his car. He seemed totally unconcerned about our mysterious package."

"Small blessings. Well, pray first and about everything. Let us entreat the good Lord to give us wisdom and guidance. Our Father," he began, "we need your help again. Mr. McCoy is so consumed with greed that he has already hurt Mary. We pray for Mary's healing and protection as you lead us through this present danger. Please send your angel armies to surround us. We pray for wisdom in the solving of Captain Smith's puzzle. You have put us here for your divine purpose in this time and place. We are your obedient servants. Please lead us, our mighty God. We ask these things in the holy name of Jesus, our Savior. Amen."

"Amen," echoed Maggie. Reverend Jim rose from the table and went to the stove. He lifted a saucepan lid and checked the noodles.

"Good here." He lifted the other lid on the tomato sauce. Breathing in the burst of steam as it escaped, he added, "Also done." Checking the skillet, he quickly flipped the contents before returning it to the burner. "Not quite done. A few minutes more, I think." He clicked the saucepan burners off.

Once more, he sat at the table and then said, "Curare again, I think."

Maggie paused thoughtfully. "It could work. We know he's interested in coming through the cellar door. But what if he's talked to Weyer and is wise to us?"

"No worries there, my dear. McCoy has no clue what happened to Mr. Weyer. For that matter, Mr. Weyer doesn't know what happened himself. Did I tell you that I visited him in prison?"

"No, you didn't."

"Yes, our Donovan Weyer is rather rough around the edges—bad language and all that. But we did have a good talk. As the saying goes, you can't judge a book by its cover."

"'The LORD does not look at the things man looks at. Man looks at the outward appearance, but the LORD looks at the heart' (1 Samuel 16:7)," quoted Maggie.

"The anointing of David. Yes, very apropos. Not that Mr. Weyer is a David, mind you, but there is more to him than meets the eye."

Once again at the stove, Reverend Jim checked the skillet and said, "Done! Let's put the lasagna together."

Maggie rose from her chair. She moved the baking dish to the counter beside the stove. Reverend Jim moved to the sink and then emptied most of the water from the pan. He skillfully lifted and placed the pasta ribbons in the dish in neat rows. Then came the layer of tomato sauce, mushroom mixture, and cheese. Layer by layer, they filled the pan. "Now, a light dusting of Parmesan on the top, and into the oven it goes!"

Returning to the table, Reverend Jim continued, "The cellar door handles might work, you know if you can somehow stick him with a sharp coated in curare. That way, he won't make it into the house."

"That might be a little too much in Mr. Butler's view. He sees quite a bit from that front window, but you're on the right track. The basement stairs railing or door, maybe both. They could hold a needle, but it would have to be inconspicuous. He'll probably have a flashlight."

"Excellent, and until nightfall, I think it might be wise to borrow an idea from Mr. Holmes. We could initiate the Maple Street Gang to keep watch on the silver car and, thus, track McCoy's whereabouts."

"Yes," Maggie added, intrigued by the idea. "Let's run it by Monk and the others during lunch."

"With the intelligence from the Maple Street Gang," said Reverend Jim, "we can better predict when our Mr. McCoy will arrive AND be ready for his visit." At this, he raised his hands toward Heaven and said, "Thank you, our God, King of the angel armies. You have answered our prayers. Please continue to safeguard and lead us."

"Amen," closed Maggie. "He always provides!"

The backdoor opened, and Monk, Tommy, Derek, and Larry entered.

"What smells so good?" asked Derek.

"Only Reverend Jim's famous lasagna," answered Maggie. Four gigantic smiles lit the faces of the young men. "During lunch, Reverend Jim and I have an idea to bounce off y'all."

Monk smiled. "We'll wash up then."

As the young men left the kitchen, Reverend Jim said in a raised voice, "It'll be ready in about fifteen minutes."

Maggie set the table for six while Reverend Jim slipped a cookie sheet with the heavily buttered garlic bread into the oven and turned on the broiler.

In due time, the boys again entered the kitchen, taking in the smells of the lasagna and garlic bread. Reverend Jim retrieved the delectable dishes from the oven, where they'd been left to keep warm. He set the lasagna with a serving spoon on a trivet on the table, then slid the garlic bread into a bun warmer beside it.

As those around the table bowed their heads, Reverend Jim began the blessing: "Father, for this food, fellowship, health, and wisdom, we give you thanks. We praise you and worship you, our God. Amen."

At the close of the prayer, the young men quickly held up plates to Reverend Jim, who served generous portions of bread and lasagna. With the plates once again in front of them, the boys took a second to inhale the delicious smell before digging in.

"Reverend Jim and I have a little job for 'The Maple Street Gang,'" Maggie began. All four teenagers looked up from their plates with interest. "There is a certain person we want you to keep track of for the rest of today."

"McCoy?" queried Monk.

"Precisely. We fully expect he will pay a little visit here tonight. To make certain that the greeting we have planned for him goes as smoothly as possible, we need to keep an eye on him for the rest of the day. Are y'all interested?"

"I'd say!" said Tommy. The others nodded eagerly in agreement.

"We need to be updated rather regularly, I'm afraid," added Reverend Jim.

Looking at Larry, Monk exclaimed, "We could use the walkie-talkies!"

"Yeah! That's a great idea!" answered Larry.

"We'll take care of it," said Monk to Maggie. "It's that silver car, correct?" Maggie nodded. "I noticed it following you from the hobby shop. We'll work out a surveillance plan and start right after lunch. Don't worry. We'll cover the whole town."

Maggie smiled and Reverend Jim interjected, "Just remember it needs to be covert. McCoy can't suspect we're on to him." The boys all nodded. "The great thing about this scheme is that you guys will look like teenagers on summer break."

"That gives me an idea," said Tommy. We'll give one of the radios to Reverend Jim so he can hear all the conversations. If we involve a few more kids from church, we could form four groups, each with its own walkie-talkie. We won't look suspicious with props like basketballs, skateboards, and boomboxes."

"Would it be all right if we ate in the living room?" asked Monk. "That way, we could plan this whole thing out and use the phone to recruit some friends."

"By all means. Just remember—"

"We know. No messes," the boys chorused as they gathered their plates.

"Oh, Monk," continued Maggie. "Would you ask Dodie to stop by the manse after she gets off work? I've got a little job for her to do."

"Sure thing," came his reply as the boys moved into the living room.

Chapter

XIII

THE MAPLE STREET GANG

After lunch, Reverend Jim led the lads home, and the Maple Street Gang left to begin their surveillance of Max McCoy. Maggie sat at the kitchen table, contemplating the evening ahead.

The first thing to do is figure out where and how to place the items to inject the curare. She rose from her chair and stretched before gathering the dirty dishes from the table and putting them into the sink. As she tidied up from lunch, she busied her mind by walking through possible scenarios.

When the work was completed, she walked down the hallway to the basement door and opened it. She turned on the light at the top of the stairs and then walked down the steps. At the bottom, she turned and began slowly back up the stairs.

Oh, wait! What is McCoy's dominant hand? That determines where to place the sharp coated in curare. Her mind reflected back to when she had observed him smoking beside his car. *That's right, the cigarette was in his right hand.*

Eyeing the handrail, she tried several times to hold it with her right hand as she placed a foot on the first step. *The main pressure of the hand is in the palm, but putting the curare on the top of the handrail makes it highly visible. If McCoy has a light, which he likely will, he'll surely notice it.* She then looked at her thumb as it grasped the rail. *Yes, that's a possibility, but I still can't be sure WHERE he will hold the handrail.*

Moving back to the top of the stairs, she eyed the doorknob. *This might work, but it must be placed on the backside to avoid detection.* She placed her hand on the knob and began to turn it, noticing where her fingers contacted the backside.

She descended the stairs once more, looking at them carefully. They were simply constructed, consisting only of treads and runners, but no risers. *Wait a minute! The stairs are open, providing me with access to McCoy's legs and ankles from below.* She moved a narrow table against the back of the staircase.

An old oilcloth cover on the top hung about eight inches off the sides. She slid the tablecloth over the side nearest the stairs so that it touched the floor. She then crouched behind the table and slowly stood up. *Yes, that might work. I'll need one of Mary's larger sewing needles to dip into the curare. One quick jab to the leg, and that should do it. I'll use the one on the doorknob as a backup.*

Maggie headed back up the steps to the hallway. She opened the utility closet door and pulled out a metal toolbox. *I see Mary still has a good supply of tools.* Rummaging through the box, she pulled out a small cardboard rectangle punched through with upholstery tacks. *This should work nicely with some duct tape to secure it!* Eyeing a roll of the silver-colored tape in the box, she removed it and tore off a small piece. She pushed the point of one of the tacks through the duct tape, sticky side down, and flush to its base. She then taped the tack to the back of the basement doorknob. *It works! Thank you, Father!*

Satisfied with the plan, Maggie replaced the tacks and tape in the toolbox and then returned it to the closet. *I'll have time to set things up before dark. I think it best not to have the curare set out until just before McCoy arrives. Now, off to the manse!*

Maggie left through the back door, checking to ensure it was locked. She made her way through the hedge and, within minutes, knocked on Reverend Jim's front door.

"What kept you?" said the kind clergyman as he opened the door.

Entering the foyer and waiting for the door to close, she responded, "The placement of the curare, but I've got that worked out now."

"Good!" Shadrach and Meshach, hearing a familiar voice, rushed to Maggie with wagging tails. Kneeling to their level, she rubbed them behind their ears and necks.

"And I expect you two to do your part tonight."

Reverend Jim laughed. "Oh, don't worry. I think they sense the excitement."

Standing up, Maggie replied, "I'm sure!"

Jim motioned for her to enter the living room. "And why are we involving Dodie specifically, may I ask?"

Maggie paused to sit down in a comfortable armchair. "Because she is just about my height and build."

"Oh. I see."

"We need to convince McCoy that the house is empty. However, it is essential that I remain inside. I'll get Dodie to dress in one of my outfits and have her leave with you and the boys in full view of McCoy. He should believe that Dodie is me."

"Very clever, Miss North."

Pointing upward, she replied, "The credit goes to God alone." Just then, a crackle was heard from one of the side tables.

"This is Engineer Bill to Sinbad. Sinbad, are you there? Over."

Maggie looked surprised at first and then began to laugh. Reverend Jim picked up the walkie-talkie from the side table. Pushing in the switch, he responded, "This is Sinbad. How is the train ride coming, Engineer Bill? Over."

"The ride is fine, but the train is coming up on a switch in the track. Boy, I could use a slice of pie about now. Over."

"Roger that, Engineer Bill," came another voice. "This is Simple Simon. I'm headed to the pie man now. Over."

Reverend Jim set the walkie-talkie back on the side table. "That's..," he began.

"Larry," Maggie finished. "And Engineer Bill is Tommy, correct, Sinbad the Sailor?"

"Pretty clever, those boys. They thought it best to use code names. Derek is Mantis. That's because he likes to collect insects, and Monk is Motorcycle McQueen. Currently, Tommy has handed off surveillance to Larry, who is near Shoofly Pies. That indicates McCoy has headed to that part of town."

"I must say, I'm very impressed," beamed Maggie.

"Even the lads have code names," Reverend Jim laughed. "They're the Dynamic Duo!" At this, Maggie knelt beside the dogs again and petted their heads.

"And that they are!" Glancing at the carriage clock on the mantle, she continued, "Dodie should be here soon."

"Oh, wait, you mean the Masked Squirrel?"

Maggie laughed. "I can see how well they've planned this out."

"You'd better believe it, Ninja from the North."

"Oh, I like that!" she replied heartily, rising to her feet.

"In all seriousness, what did you decide about the trap?"

"Yes, back to business. I'm utilizing some of Mary's upholstery tacks, duct tape, and sewing notions. First,

I'll tape a tack coated in curare to the backside of the doorknob. Then, I'll be at the bottom of the stairs with a large sewing needle for a surprise attack."

Just then, the radio crackled to life again. "Simple Simon to Mantis. Over."

"Mantis here. How's the pie? Over."

"A silver fly landed on my pie, but I shooed it away. Over."

"I see one coming my way. I'll catch it for you. Over."

Reverend Jim translated: "McCoy has passed by the bakery and is headed toward the park. Derek and his crew are there under the guise of collecting insects."

"I see," responded Maggie.

"Motorcycle McQueen to Sinbad. Over," came Monk's voice from the radio.

"Sinbad here. Over," responded Reverend Jim.

"I just saw the Masked Squirrel run across the telephone wires to a nearby tree. Maybe it's pursuing the Ninja from the North? Over."

"Message relayed. Sinbad over and out."

Looking at Maggie, Reverend Jim continued, "That means Dodie is almost here, and I'm to let you know."

Within a few seconds, the door chime sounded, and Shadrach and Meshach hurried to the foyer and sat down, waiting patiently for Reverend Jim. As he opened the front door, he greeted Dodie. "Come in, come in! He commanded the lads to accompany them to the living room.

"Thank you, Reverend Jim. I understand from Monk that y'all need my help."

Maggie greeted the Masked Squirrel from the living room. "Hi, Dodie. Thank you for coming and for your willingness to help. In short, I need you to impersonate me this evening."

"Intriguing. Does this have something to do with the guys hanging out around town this afternoon?"

"Yes. You know we caught Mary's attacker?"

"Mr. Weyer, yes. He's in jail now."

"Correct. Well, we found out that he was hired by someone else. That someone has now arrived in Kevan's Cove—"

"And poses a threat to Mary and Monk," finished Dodie.

"Exactly. We've worked out a little plan to catch our unwanted visitor, but I need him to believe everyone is out of the house this evening. Which is where you come in."

"Got it. You can count me in."

"Great. I'm headed back to Mary's house. Reverend Jim will help sneak you inside the house shortly."

With that, Maggie quickly hugged Dodie and then conspicuously left the manse. Instead of taking the back entrance through the hedge, she strode down the sidewalk in front of the house. She followed the driveway to the back door and then went inside.

Chapter

XIV

THE FELLER IN THE CELLAR

"**O** Father," prayed Maggie, "as you did for King David in 1 Samuel 17:47, I ask that you once again give us victory so that 'All those gathered here will know that it is not by sword or spear that the LORD saves; for the battle is the LORD's, and he will give all of you into our hands.' Guide my hands, give me stealth, grant to us all your protection. I ask these things in Jesus' name. Amen."

Maggie quickly moved into action, retrieving the tacks and duct tape from the hall closet. She then went to the back bedroom where Mary kept her sewing machine. Beside the machine was a small box containing sewing notions. Maggie lifted the lid and quickly found what she was looking for. Holding a long sewing needle between her thumb and index finger, she lifted it to the light from the window. *Definitely sharp enough!* Noticing a spool of button thread, she took a pair of scissors from the box and snipped off a long piece.

She brought all the items to the kitchen table and assembled the night's weapons. First, she tore a strip of duct tape from the roll and ripped it in half. Then, she punctured the tape with an upholstery tack so the adhesive side was opposite the tack's point.

Maggie now turned her focus to the sewing needle. She held the button thread in her thumb and index finger, then moistened the end with her lips. Holding the needle in the opposite hand, she slowly guided the thread into the eye and pulled it through. Once both loose ends of the thread were even, she tied a knot.

Now, to make this a little easier to hold. Grabbing the remaining strip of duct tape, she wrapped it around the needle's eye and button thread all the way to the knot. She held the completed weapon in her hand and smiled. *That will work nicely! And now for the curare!*

She walked to the living room couch and lifted one of her duffle bags from behind it. She unzipped the top, opening the bag wide. Pushing the contents to one side, she exposed the bottom seam of the bag. Pulling apart a hook and loop fastener, she revealed a hidden pocket containing a small bottle.

Maggie took her completed projects and the curare bottle to the hallway and then opened the basement door. She stepped down to the first step and turned around. As before, she reached to open the door, noticing where her right hand touched the knob.

Identifying a location on the back of the knob, she took the tack, opened the curare bottle, then dipped the sharp point in until it was well coated. Replacing the lid, she slipped the container into her pants pocket. Carefully holding the ends of the tape, she attached it to the knob, ensuring that it wasn't easily seen. *I won't coat the other sharp until just before McCoy gets here.*

She walked down to the bottom of the stairs, ducking behind them to the narrow table she had set up earlier. She lifted a corner of the oilcloth and pushed the needle under and back through it. *That will keep it in place until I'm ready to arm it.*

She ascended to the top of the stairs in time to hear a quick rap on the back door.

Reverend Jim and the lads were the first to enter. Four teenagers huddled around the back steps, with Dodie concealed in the middle. She covertly entered through the doorway, followed by Monk, Tommy, and then Larry. The teenagers excitedly recounted their day's adventure to Dodie, who listened intently and smiled.

"A stern word of warning," interrupted Maggie. "Do not open the basement door." The conversation stopped briefly as the teenagers turned to look at her. "The less you know, the better, but please, do not go near the basement." They nodded and picked up their conversation once more. Maggie motioned to Dodie to join her in the living room. "Thanks again, Dodie, for your willingness to help."

"It sounds like I've already missed out on a lot," she laughed. Maggie lifted a second duffle bag from near the couch and then removed a pair of blue denim overalls and a light blue t-shirt.

"The bathroom is at the end of the hall. Change into these while I get my bike gear." Dodie left for the bathroom while Maggie walked to the hallway. She opened the coat closet door and removed her leather jacket, boots, gloves, and helmet.

Noticing that Dodie was conspicuously absent from the kitchen, Monk entered the hallway just in time to see her emerge, dressed in Maggie's clothes.

"Hey, those look great on you!"

Dodie imitated a model's walk and turn before breaking into a big smile. "Thanks, Monk. I like them a lot."

"And here," said Maggie, returning to the living room, "is my gear. Now, this is the plan. Monk, you and Dodie will leave the house in full gear. With helmets on, McCoy should mistake Dodie for me. Here are the keys to Magers. Take Dodie to Reverend Jim's, but go in a round-about-manner so McCoy thinks you're leaving for a while."

"Got it."

"Reverend Jim and the guys will walk back and meet you there. By the way, where was McCoy last located?"

"At the diner. Derek, or should I say, Mantis, is keeping an eye on him."

"Good." Walking back to the kitchen, the three rejoined the group. "Thanks for the use of the lads again, Reverend Jim."

"You know, I think they look forward to coming over here. Visiting Mary's house now means an adventure!"

Maggie laughed nervously. "I'll be glad when this part is done. Pray for me."

"Always." Just then, four radios crackled to life with Derek's voice.

"Mantis to Sinbad. Over."

Reverend Jim picked up one of the radios and then replied, "Sinbad here. Over."

"I've finished collecting insects, but the prized one got away. He flew up into a maple tree. Over."

"We'll help you sort your collection. Sinbad over and out. Alright, that's our cue. McCoy is almost here."

Reverend Jim handed Maggie a walkie-talkie. "Here you go, my girl. Please let us know when he's down. Until then, it'll be radio silence."

Tommy, who had been watching out the window, turned to the group. "He's here, parked across the street. Maggie, you'd better get into position before we leave."

"Thanks, Tommy. I'm headed to the basement with Shadrach and Meshach."

"Let's go, you guys," he continued. "Remember to act normal!" With that, the group left the house. Monk and Dodie, as planned, left on the bike while the others strode down the driveway before turning right onto the sidewalk.

As the evening sky darkened, the pole light from the carport shone through the basement windows, dimly illuminating the room. Now in place behind the stairs, Maggie whispered to the lads, "Shadrach, Meshach, quiet." They obediently sat nearby without making a sound.

Shining a small light on the table, she removed the needle. Reaching into her pocket, she retrieved the small bottle. After unscrewing the lid, Maggie delicately dipped the needle point into the curare. She replaced the lid before slipping the container back into her pocket. Then she carefully held the needle firmly between her thumb, index, and middle fingers with the tape tail pressed to her palm with her ring and pinky fingers. She nervously switched off the flashlight. *Please help me, Father. Guide my hand!*

McCoy didn't waste any time. Within minutes of the group leaving, Maggie heard the metal cellar door creaking, followed by slow, even footsteps descending the concrete stairs. The beam from a flashlight broke through the darkness as McCoy moved the light from side to side, gaining his bearings as he searched for a way to the upper story.

Maggie slowly waved her hands at the lads to get their attention. Shaping her hands into fists, she lifted them slightly, signaling Shadrach and Meshach. They rose to their feet, standing perfectly still, and waited for the intruder to get closer.

Spotting the wooden stairs, McCoy made his way through the basement and slowly began to ascend the steps with his flashlight aimed at the top of the staircase. As the wooden treads creaked, Maggie carefully rose from behind the table. *Wait for it—one more tread. Go!*

With boldness, she grabbed the ankle in front of her with her left hand while jabbing the prepared needle into it with her right. The needle easily pierced the intruder's thin, summer-weight trousers, puncturing the skin above the ankle. McCoy let out a wail, partly from surprise and partly from pain.

Maggie quickly grabbed his heel with her left hand and pulled it firmly, causing him to lose his balance and drop the flashlight. Within seconds, he lay at the bottom of the stairs, very much awake but unable to move because of the curare.

"Lads, guard!" Shadrach and Meshach rushed to the intruder and then began circling and growling at the terrified man. Using McCoy's dropped flashlight, Maggie found the light switch and snapped it on.

Grabbing the radio from her pocket, she pushed the button. "Ninja from the North to Sinbad. Bug squashed. Over and out."

Chapter

A Puzzle in Plain Sight

In the few minutes it took Reverend Jim and the Maple Street Gang to arrive, Maggie had McCoy securely bound and gagged. She removed the tack from the doorknob and then carefully wiped it and the needle to remove any trace of curare. Shadrach and Meshach, who had ceased guarding at Maggie's command, sat near McCoy's head, looking him intently in the eye.

One quick rummage through his pockets before the police take him away, she thought. *Maybe I'll find another clue.* Maggie knelt and then quickly searched McCoy's pants and shirt pockets, but to no avail.

Just then, her eye caught sight of a small notebook that had fallen near the stairs. Its black cover was well-worn. She picked it up and then tucked it in her overalls' front pocket. As she rose, she heard Reverend Jim's voice from the top of the stairs.

"Praise be to our magnificent God!"

"Yes," responded Maggie. "It wasn't by my strength, for certain. He fought for us. By the by, would you phone the police? Oh, and keep the gang up there until the police haul this one away."

"Consider it done."

Maggie looked around the basement, resting her eye on the narrow table under the stairs. She pulled the tablecloth back to the center and ran her hands across it to smooth the fabric. Now, everything appeared back to normal.

She ascended the stairs to the utility closet and quickly put away the tack in the toolbox. *I'll leave the sewing needle with the tack until I have time to clean them thoroughly.* After shutting the closet door, she returned to the basement.

The Kevan's Cove police department beat their previous record. The same two officers who arrested Weyer soon descended the basement stairs and stood looking at McCoy.

"Caught another one, I see," said the older officer.

"Yes. He was breaking in through the cellar door."

"Yep, we noticed one of the doors still open."

"I was already in the basement when I heard it open, so I hid behind the stairs. I'm grateful the dogs were here. Once again, they did most of the work."

Lifting McCoy to his feet, the younger officer replaced the rope with handcuffs and then led the dazed man out of the cellar door.

"I think that's all we need for now," said the older officer.

"Thank you. I appreciate your help!"

The officer tipped his hat as he left through the cellar doors, closing them before leaving. Waiting patiently for Maggie's command, Shadrach and Meshach voiced soft whines of excitement.

"I'm sorry, lads! At ease." With those words, the pair quickly climbed the basement steps toward the sound of their master's voice. Maggie followed into the living room to find Reverend Jim kneeling on the floor with his arms around both dogs.

"Good job, lads, well done!" The dog's short tails wagged enthusiastically at the praise. "Well, Maggie, my child, now we have a puzzle to solve." At this comment, Dodie spoke up.

"I've heard bits and pieces of this from the guys, but would you explain what's going on? Why was Mary attacked?" Maggie looked at Monk, encouraging him to answer.

"We think we've found part of the answer to that from the information you gave us in the deed search, Dodie. Captain Smith built this house and lived here until his mysterious death. We think he hid something valuable in the house, leaving directions to it in the model ship that used to sit on the mantel."

"Mary was hurt because she surprised Donovan Weyer, who broke in to search for the hiding place. Evidently, he and his employer, Max McCoy, knew nothing about the ship and its flags. That's why they didn't know where to look."

"But y'all do, right?"

"Yes, but there's more to it," Maggie interjected. "What are the directions again, Reverend Jim?" He moved to the mantle and then turned with his back to it.

"This is where Captain Smith was standing in the photo. Let's see. Nine, right, five, left, one. I'm going to try paces for the numbers, which is about thirty inches per pace." He counted off nine paces from the fireplace.

"Hey," said Tommy enthusiastically, "turning right sends you down the hallway!"

Reverend Jim turned and counted off another five paces, passing by the staircase. The teenagers eagerly followed. At the last step, he turned left and then took one final pace. His nose almost touched the wall beneath the staircase.

Larry, squatting on the floor, pointed to the wall. "Why are there two outlets so close together?"

Monk's eyes widened. "Miss Mary said the left one has never worked! Quick, a slotted screwdriver!"

"On it," Maggie said as she left the room. She quickly returned with the toolbox from the utility closet. "Just to make sure it isn't hot, plug the table lamp into the outlet."

Monk did as requested. The bulb remained dark. He tried its twin with the same result. Maggie handed him the screwdriver. He swiftly removed the cover plate and then the false receptacle. Smiling, he held it up for the others to see. There were no wires connected!

"Well," began Derek after a pause, "what is in there?"

"It's too dark to tell."

Maggie, remembering the light in her pocket, handed it to Monk. He snapped it on and then peered into the opening.

"It's some sort of lever." Reaching into the open space, Monk pushed upward. Suddenly, there was a "clunk" from inside the staircase.

Tommy spoke for the group when he asked, "What was that?"

"A hidden compartment somewhere in the staircase," postulated Reverend Jim. "But where and how do we find it?"

"I know this isn't the best timing," replied Maggie, "but it's getting late, and I'm tired. Besides, I think I know someone who can help us solve this."

Turning to Monk, she said, "You take Dodie home." Dodie waved goodbye as she and Monk walked to the kitchen, then out the back door.

Larry piped up. "Would it be alright if we stayed over? We'll call our parents and all."

"Yes, that's fine. I'll take Mary's room. Y'all can camp out here in the living room, and Reverend Jim will be over bright and early to help with breakfast, right?"

"Right," came his reply. Moving to the kitchen, he leashed the lads then said, "Goodnight," as they left through the back door.

"Goodnight," replied the three boys.

While Larry, Derek, and Tommy called their parents, Maggie retrieved blankets, sheets, and pillows from an upstairs linen closet. She placed them on the sofa when she returned to the living room.

"Any chance of a snack before bed," asked Larry.

Maggie smiled and agreed, "All of this excitement has made me hungry, too. There should be some cookies in the pantry."

She entered the kitchen, followed by three hungry teenagers. Maggie reached into the pantry, removed a blue willow tin, and then set it on the table, followed by glasses and a carton of milk. "Help yourselves. I've got a call to make."

Maggie walked to the living room telephone table and then removed the phone directory from the drawer. She flipped through its pages until she found the entry for "Davis' Garage." She picked up the phone receiver and then dialed the number.

"Hi. Is this Brad? Hi, Brad. I'm glad I caught you before you closed. This is Maggie North, the one with the sidecar outfit. That's right. I have a favor to ask. My friends and I have a puzzle to solve involving architecture. Would you be able to help us out tomorrow morning? Great. What time and where should I pick you up? Got it. Thank you, Brad. Goodnight." She replaced the receiver into its cradle.

"Who is Brad?" queried Larry once Maggie had returned to the kitchen.

"A new acquaintance I met on the way here. He's studying architecture at college."

128

"Then he might be able to figure out where the hidden recess is!"

"Exactly. I'm grateful that God crossed our paths."

The backdoor opened, and Monk entered the kitchen, eyeing the cookies and milk on the table.

"Dodie's home safe."

"Good," replied Maggie.

"She really enjoyed riding in the sidecar," beamed Monk as he hung the bike keys on a nail by the door.

Maggie smiled. "I've got an errand for you and Magers tomorrow morning." Monk looked up, interested. "Do you know Davis' Garage, about fifteen minutes outside town?"

"Yeah, I know the place."

"Brad Davis will be there at eight o'clock tomorrow morning."

Tommy answered Monk's confused look, "He's majoring in architecture at college."

"Oh, then he can help!"

"Exactly," replied Maggie as she dunked an oatmeal and raisin cookie into a glass of cold milk. "We are very blessed, gentlemen. God is bringing all the pieces of this puzzle together."

Heads nodded in agreement around the table. After a few seconds, Larry broke the silence. "I'm so excited. I don't think I'll be able to sleep a wink tonight."

Derek chided, "You'll be the first one asleep, as usual!" All four friends laughed.

"I know I won't have any trouble falling asleep," added Maggie. "I'm exhausted." She rose from the table, moved to the sink, and rinsed her glass. "I'll see y'all in the morning. Goodnight."

The four friends contentedly ate cookies while recounting the night's events and hypothesizing about the location and contents of the hidden compartment. The clock ticked away while the number of cookies dwindled. Finally, Monk said, "Hey, we need to get to bed. I've got to get up early."

The boys cleared the table and rinsed their glasses.

Within minutes of brushing their teeth, all four were sound asleep on the living room floor.

Chapter

XVI

THE SECRET UNDER THE STAIRS

Early morning found Maggie at the kitchen table. The smell of fresh coffee filled the room. Her Bible was open to 1 Peter 5:6-7, "Humble yourselves, therefore, under God's mighty hand, that he may lift you up in due time. Cast all your anxiety on him because he cares for you." The passage had been underlined twice.

Father, thank you for last night's victory. You, indeed, are mighty! Whatever today brings, I am so grateful that you love me. Please keep me humble. Amen. Raising her bowed head, she drank a sip of hot coffee and leaned back in her chair, resting.

"Good morning," whispered Monk as he entered the kitchen, making his way to the stove for a cup of coffee.

"How'd you sleep?"

"I feel," he paused, "I don't know…free. Watching how God worked this out has made me realize that I just need to trust him with everything."

He took a seat at the table. Maggie squeezed his hand in reassurance. "That's right, Monk. It's that simple. Understanding that God is in control of our lives is freeing. I used to try to make things work, like the fabled stepsisters and the shoe. I arrogantly tried to force my future into a life that would never give me peace. But oh, when I let go, wow! That's when my life really began."

"Thank you for coming, Maggie. I can't tell you how much I appreciate it." Glancing at the clock, he rose from the table and then grabbed the bike keys from the nail by the door. "I'd better head out to pick up Brad. Tell Reverend Jim to save some breakfast for me."

"Will do." Again, Maggie leaned back in her chair and watched the rising sun from the kitchen window, enjoying the quiet of the morning.

Suddenly, she remembered the small black notebook from last night. Rising from her chair, she quietly walked through the living room and then up the stairs to Mary's room. Unfastening the front pocket of her black overalls, she reached in and pulled out the notebook. She then quietly returned to the kitchen and her cup of coffee.

Carefully opening the book, she scanned its yellowed pages for clues. *It's a diary of sorts. Let's see.* She began to read the contents. "April 15, 1965: Last sail along the coast. Retire tomorrow. April 16, 1965: Found it!" *Found what?* She flipped a few pages, then continued. "March 8, 1970: Hidden in the house." *What is McCoy doing with Captain Smith's diary? Better yet, what did Captain Smith hide?*

"Are they up yet?" came Reverend Jim's voice from the back door. "I come bearing provisions."

"Not yet. Is that bread I smell?"

"I couldn't sleep last night. So, while I worked on the puzzle of the outlet, I made two loaves."

"Any progress?"

"Well, I have two loaves," he laughed. "For the puzzle, not much progress there. It must be something inside the staircase, but I don't recall any way to access that space."

Moving to the living room, he shouted, "Time to rise and shine!" Three sleepy teenagers slowly sat up and rubbed their eyes. "Wash up. Breakfast will be ready soon."

"French toast, I'm hoping?" queried Maggie as he returned to the kitchen.

"Yes, French toast." With that, Reverend Jim collected a mixing bowl and an eggbeater from a cabinet. Then, he retrieved the ingredients from the pantry and refrigerator. "I brought a dozen eggs since I wasn't certain how many were left." He handed Maggie a bread knife and cutting board and added, "Even slices, please."

"Certainly." Reverend Jim cracked the eggs into the bowl as Maggie sliced the bread. He then poured in the milk and vanilla extract, and added cinnamon. Using the manual eggbeater, he whipped the mixture until it was foamy.

As he removed a long, cast-iron griddle from a side cabinet, he asked, "How did you sleep?"

"Like a baby! Knowing that McCoy is behind bars put my mind at ease."

Rev. Jim placed the griddle on the stove and lit two burners. He slathered butter across the top of the griddle. "Alright, my dear, I'll take some of those slices now." He dipped each slice into the egg mixture and then placed it on the griddle.

"McCoy is bad news, especially if he killed Captain Smith, as we suspect."

"That is the one thing that has been bugging me. What in this house is worth taking someone's life?"

Maggie rose and began setting the table. "McCoy had the captain's diary. I found it last night." She retrieved the small notebook from the table and handed it to the clergyman.

She continued, "It's a bit cryptic, though, but the captain did hide something. In the diary, he only said it was in the house. It confirms my suspicion that McCoy must have searched the Rhode Island house in vain until he found out about the captain's place here in Kevan's Cove. Anyway, I'm glad he's safely behind bars."

"That man has a dark heart, my dear," he said. After glancing through its pages, he returned the notebook to Maggie. Turning to the stove, he neatly flipped the bread slices.

"Oh, don't forget to set some aside for Monk and Brad. They'll be back soon."

"Mmm! French toast!" Tommy was the first to appear. "I'll get the syrup." Larry and Derek followed, inhaling the sweet cinnamon smell. Maggie poured coffee while Reverend Jim placed two nicely browned slices on each plate.

After everyone was seated, he asked, "Derek, would you say the blessing?"

"Yes, Reverend Jim." Everyone bowed their heads as Derek prayed, "Heavenly Father, thank you for this breakfast, great friends, and this amazing adventure. Be with us today, give us wisdom, and help us solve Captain Smith's puzzle. Amen."

Multiple "Amens" echoed the prayer.

"Monk sure was up early," observed Larry.

"Speaking of," replied Maggie, "he should be back any minute." As if on cue, they all heard the roar of Magersfontein's engine in the drive. Within minutes, Brad and Monk were seated at the kitchen table with the others, enjoying French toast with coffee.

Monk made introductions between bites, after which Tommy filled Brad in on the details of the last few days.

"Wow!" said Brad. That's some adventure. Just to recap, you heard a clunk when the lever was turned in the outlet?"

"Yes," answered Reverend Jim. "Nothing else."

"Well then, let's take a look at the staircase." Brad led the group to the hallway. "The directions in the flag code led you about here?" Reverend Jim nodded.

Brad looked at the entire length of the wall and then began tapping on it. "Hmm, I wonder." He walked up the staircase, stopping at the first landing. He rolled up the area rug that covered the hardwood floor, then crouched down to get a closer look. "Yes!"

"What did you find?" asked Monk in an excited voice.

"There is an outline of a rectangle here in the floor and," he paused, tracing the shape with his finger, "there's a keyhole—"

"The key! That's where it fits!" Maggie broke in. Reverend Jim, followed by the group, joined Brad on the landing. He reached into his pocket, removed the key that had been hidden in the model ship's mast, and then handed it to Brad.

"That looks right," continued Brad. He fitted the key into the small keyhole concealed in a wooden knot. It fit! He turned the key and then used it as a handle to lift the wooden hatch. Answering the others' looks of amazement, he continued, "These secret rooms were very popular during Prohibition. They used them to hide illegal spirits."

"Of course!" said Maggie. "Old Captain Smith would have known all about that kind of thing!"

"Any chance of a flashlight?" asked Brad.

"The one from last night is still on the telephone table," replied Monk.

Tommy jumped up. "I'll get it," he said, running down the stairs. He quickly returned and handed it to Brad. With the flashlight on, Brad peered inside the hidden room.

"I don't think anyone's been in here for quite a while. Plenty of cobwebs."

Maggie skipped down the stairs and around the corner. She quickly returned with a broom in hand.

"There's a ladder here," continued Brad.

"Spiders first," said Maggie.

"Spiders," laughed the teenagers.

"They won't hurt you!" retorted Larry.

Maggie looked up with a sternness in her eyes, "I don't care for spiders."

"Actually," interjected Derek, "some around here are dangerous."

"And they get in your hair," she shuddered. Maggie leaned over the opening, sweeping the space with the broom to remove decades of cobwebs and dust. "Shine the light there, Brad. I think it's a light." The beam of the flashlight illuminated an antique porcelain pull chain fixture.

"Alright, the broom and I are going in." Maggie nimbly descended the wooden ladder. At the bottom, she pulled on the beaded chain. Instantly, the small chamber was flooded with light.

"I'm headed down, too," said Brad as he descended the ladder. Inside the staircase, rustic wooden shelves covered the walls. "The outlet is nearest this set of shelves," he said as he crouched on the floor. He paused, "Oh, now that's clever." The opening above was suddenly full of faces as everyone wanted to see what Brad was talking about. Maggie sat on her heels, peering under the bottom shelf.

"Oh, wow! It's built out from the wall but hidden by the shelf."

"What is it?" asked Larry with excitement.

"I think it's the answer to what went clunk last night," replied Maggie. The lever unlocked this hidden cabinet."

As she grasped the edge of the front panel, it swung open freely, revealing a small wooden chest. She handed it to Brad, who then lifted it to Reverend Jim's waiting hands.

Back at the kitchen table, the group huddled around Reverend Jim, who was dusting the box with a handkerchief. "I'm no expert," the clergyman said, "but this is old." He tried to lift the metal latch, but it was stiff from lack of oil. Monk ran to the carport and quickly returned with a metal oil can.

Reverend Jim squirted oil on the hinges of the latch and used a pocket knife to work it open. Taking a deep breath, he lifted the lid. Everyone gasped. The box contained silver and gold coins, precious gems, and exquisite jewelry.

"Pirate's treasure!" shouted Tommy.

Maggie slowly spoke, "This is what Captain Smith found just before he retired from sailing. He moved to Kevan's Cove, built this house, and hid the treasure inside the staircase." She paused, then said, "Poor Mary. McCoy would have killed her for this."

"Now, now," comforted Reverend Jim. "'I took you from the ends of the earth, from its farthest corners I called you. I said, "You are my servant"; I have chosen you and have not rejected you. So do not fear, for I am with you; do not be dismayed, for I am your God. I will strengthen you and help you; I will uphold you with my righteous right hand'" (Isaiah 41:9-10). He added, "Always remember, God is in control."

Chapter

XVII

MARY'S HOMECOMING

"How much is this worth?" asked Derek.

"I'm not an expert," Reverend Jim said, "but I'd say a pretty penny."

"Well, if you'll excuse me, I've got a call to make," said Maggie.

Moving to the living room, she picked up the telephone receiver and then dialed. With a quiet voice, she said, "Yes, this is Maggie North. We've recovered an item of significant value. Yes. Yes. I understand. Thank you." She hung up the receiver.

Returning to the kitchen, she said, "Well, that was quite the mystery. Thank you, Brad, you proved invaluable. How did you know about the hidden room under the staircase?"

"Second semester, freshman year, I had to write a paper on creative uses of architecture. My research focused on the Prohibition era because there were so many examples. They were pretty ingenious back then!

This one was unique, though. I've never seen a hidden cabinet in one."

"It's like something right out of a Saturday morning cartoon," laughed Monk.

"Indeed," agreed Reverend Jim. "Mary comes home today, correct?" Maggie and Monk nodded. "I'm assuming this is taken care of?" he said, pointing to the box while looking at Maggie.

"Yes. They should be here soon."

"Good! Why don't the Maple Street Gang and I take Brad back, and then I'll escort these rapscallions home."

"Thank you."

"Alright, gentlemen, off we go." The group obediently followed Reverend Jim out the back door.

Maggie didn't have long to wait. A small van quietly pulled into the driveway. Maggie met two women at the backdoor and then showed them into the kitchen. The two secured the lid on the box before sliding it into a large picnic hamper and placing a colorful tablecloth on top for concealment.

"Mary will want a say in this," Maggie began. The two women nodded, lifted the hamper from the table, and carried it out the back door.

Maggie looked around the kitchen. Before Mary came home, there was a lot to do. She began washing dishes, laundering linens, vacuuming, and the like. It was well into the afternoon when Reverend Jim's car pulled into the drive.

"Oh, my child, how I have missed you!" exclaimed Miss Mary as she hugged Maggie. With tears running down her face, Maggie held tight to the woman she considered her mother. "There, there, daughter, no real harm done to the old lady."

Maggie smiled and said as Mary clasped her face between her hands, "I'm just so grateful you are back home."

"Hear, hear," chimed in Reverend Jim. "The place just hasn't been the same without you."

"So I hear! You, Jim, must make us dinner while Maggie and Monk fill me in on all the details." They entered the kitchen, where Reverend Jim gathered pots, pans, and bowls.

Maggie and Monk followed Mary into the living room. Once she was seated in her favorite armchair, they relayed the entire adventure to her.

"Well, that is quite the story! The League bought the house at auction, you know."

"No, I didn't know," replied Maggie.

"Yes, I came here soon after." Mary paused to reflect. To think that that treasure has been sitting underneath the staircase all this time." She paused, then said, "Monk, why don't you give Jim a hand with dinner? I'd like to speak with Maggie now." Monk obligingly left the room.

Maggie spoke first, "The treasure has been collected. They are waiting for your call, Mary."

"Thank you. That's what I want to discuss. It's a significant find?"

"Yes, I believe so."

"God has blessed us so that we may bless others, and that is what I intend to do. I'll make that call now." Maggie moved the phone closer to Mary's chair and handed her the receiver.

She politely headed to the kitchen. "Mmm. What's cookin'?"

"Spaghetti with garlic bread! I found more of Mary's tomato sauce in the pantry, along with leftover bread slices from breakfast. Monk is buttering the bread, so why don't you set the table?"

Before long, Mary joined them in the kitchen. "My, my, Reverend Jim, that smells delicious."

"Well, have a seat and say grace for us."

With all four seated around the table, Mary began, "Our Father, you are our Creator, the Watchman of our souls. Thank you for working all of this out for your good. Thank you for our Christian family, one of your precious treasures for us in this life. I pray that you will bless this food to our bodies. May it nourish us so that we may continue our work for your kingdom. Amen."

"Amens" followed around the table.

"And now, while we dine, I have some news to share," continued Mary. "Monk, you and your friends were very brave and of great help to Maggie and Reverend Jim. I have arranged for a college fund to be set up for each of you, including Brad Davis and Dodie." Monk's eyes widened.

Looking at Reverend Jim, she said, "And as for you, you're finally taking that fly-fishing trip to Scotland. A month's sabbatical from your duties will do you a world of good." Reverend Jim looked at her with sincere thankfulness and said, "Bless you, Mary."

"And Maggie, you're needed. They've given you just one more day here. You leave on Saturday, so you best change the oil in your bike tomorrow. You've got a long trip ahead of you."

"But she just got here," exclaimed Monk, holding back tears.

"Don't worry, Monk. You'll see her soon. That I can promise you. Now, after dinner, you call your friends. I'd like them to come over for pie and ice cream. Mrs. Williams said she'd drop a few pies by on her way home."

That evening, Mary personally thanked all the teens for their help and told them of the provisions the Magdala League had made for them. "And I've written to that nice Brad Davis to thank him."

The teenagers eagerly recounted the adventure to Mary, who lovingly listened to it all over again. Monk left the group and moved near Maggie's armchair.

"Is it okay if I help tomorrow? I'd like to learn how to change the oil."

"Absolutely! I couldn't do it without you and," she paused with a big smile, "I've got a little surprise for you." The two walked out the backdoor to the carport.

Maggie moved to a canvas-covered shape and then lifted the tarp. There, parked next to Magersfontein, was a metallic green motorcycle. Maggie handed him the keys, "Here you go!"

"It's mine? Really? But how? When?"

"It was delivered this afternoon while you were out."

"Thanks, Maggie! I can't believe this!"

"Mary and I both agree. You've earned it."

"May I take it for a ride?"

"Absolutely."

As Monk was putting on his gear, he paused. "Maggie, I wanted to ask you. Where are you going from here?"

"Oh, that? I've been called to the Southwest headquarters."

"The Southwest headquarters? Where's that?"

Smiling, Maggie responded, "Magdalena, New Mexico."

Monk chuckled. "I thought y'all tried to run under the radar. That's a rather obvious name, isn't it?"

"Sometimes it's best to hide in plain sight," she said with a smile. Monk laughed and nodded in agreement. He started the engine and let it warm up before pulling onto the street. Tommy, Derek, and Larry joined Maggie at the carport within seconds.

"Was that Monk on a bike?" queried Tommy.

Maggie nodded.

"Lucky!" responded Derek and Larry in unison.

"I think he's ready for it," Maggie mused. She paused for a moment. "Also, I understand Mary has reserved the roller rink for tomorrow afternoon. Pizza and ice cream for the whole youth group." The three young men, in high spirits, let out loud cheers.

"You'll be there, too?" asked Larry.

"Absolutely," Maggie replied. I wouldn't miss an opportunity to watch Reverend Jim roller skate!" All four were still laughing as Monk pulled into the driveway.

"What a sweet ride, Monk," began Tommy.

"It sure is a beauty," added Derek.

"How about me as a pillion?" finished Larry.

Smiling from ear to ear, Monk replied, "Thanks, fellas. And, yes, Larry, as soon as I get an extra helmet."

At this, Maggie held up her index finger. "One moment. I almost forgot." She reached into Magersfontein's sidecar and pulled out a shiny black helmet and goggles.

"Alright!" said Larry, reaching out his hand.

Just then, Dodie opened the back door and shouted. "Hey, you guys, Miss Mary wants y'all." Her eye caught sight of Monk's motorcycle. "Monk, is that yours?" Monk nodded. Walking to Maggie, Dodie grabbed the helmet and goggles and then put them on. "Alright, then, let's go!"

"Yes, ma'am," replied Monk as he sat astride the bike and again started the engine. Dodie carefully sat behind him and held on to his waist.

"Ready?" asked Monk.

"Ready." Once again, Monk carefully pulled onto the street. Maggie turned to Larry.

"I guess you didn't see that one coming, did you?" Larry shook his head and laughed. Monk and Dodie returned after their quick trip around the block.

As she removed her helmet, Dodie told Monk, "You can pick me up tomorrow for the skating party." Monk smiled and blushed.

"I'll be there at noon."

Chapter

XVIII

ROLLING IT UP AT THE RINK

Maggie was up early the following day. She started the coffee and then sat at the table reading her Bible. "Father, thank you for letting me be a part of your kingdom-building plan. Keep me riding 'victoriously on behalf of truth, humility, and righteousness' (Psalm 45:4). Thank you for your great care and your incredible love. Amen."

"Amen," chorused Mary as she entered the warm kitchen. "Just stay seated. I'll get breakfast. And before you start, yes, I'm up to it because Mrs. Williams snuck in some doughnuts with the pie delivery."

"Filled?"

"The raspberry, lemon, and chocolate are filled. There's also some plain glazed ones."

"Thank you, Mrs. Williams!"

"Indeed. It makes for an easy breakfast," laughed Mary as she placed the box of doughnuts on the table. "Save the chocolates for Monk. That's his favorite."

"Did you say chocolate doughnuts?" Monk slipped into a chair. He eagerly removed one from the box and took a bite. "Mmm."

"Here's some coffee," Mary said, setting three steaming mugs on the table. "Yes, a quick breakfast this morning. You two have some bike work to do before the skating party. And don't forget to mow the lawn. Twelve o'clock will be here before you know it, Monk." Mary winked at Maggie as she took a seat and then sipped her coffee.

As Mary predicted, the morning hours went by rapidly. Maggie showed Monk how to change the oil and service his bike. Next, they washed then waxed both motorcycles. Finally, they took turns with the push mower until the lawn was neat and trimmed.

Monk looked at his watch, "I call dibs on the shower."

"Go ahead," said Maggie. "I'm going to sit in the glider for a bit anyway." She walked up the front porch steps and plopped down onto the fluffy cushions of the glider. Closing her eyes, she gently pushed with her feet to start it swaying.

"Hello, Miss North," came a familiar voice.

Maggie opened one eye, "Why, hello, Mr. Butler. Won't you have a seat?"

"Don't mind if I do," said the elderly man as he climbed the front porch steps. "That was some excitement the other night." He took a seat on the glider next to Maggie.

Maggie turned to him and said, "I want to thank you."

"For what?"

"For keeping an eye out."

"And you can count on me to continue to do that." He paused, then said, "You're leaving, aren't you? I saw you and the boy working on the bikes."

"I'm heading out early tomorrow," she said. "The information you provided helped us catch Weyer and McCoy, so I sincerely mean thanks." As the older man smiled, Maggie continued, "That reminds me, Miss Mary has made an arrangement with Doreen at the diner. Lunch is on us for a while."

"Maggie, that's what neighbors do. We look out for each other. Besides, Mary is my sister in Christ. She's family, but I'm sad to say I have neglected that bond. When she was attacked…" He paused before adding, "Well, God convicted me of my shortcomings. Miss Mary has always reached out to me, bringing food over and inviting me to church, but I thought I was all right by myself. Now I realize that God wants his children to be a true family. Pray for me, Maggie, that I'll succeed in that."

Rising from the porch glider, he added, "And she didn't have to recompense me, but I know I'll be blessed by it. That's Miss Mary. Her heart just overflows with generosity. Well, I'm headed back across the street. I'll see you around."

"You can count on it, Mr. Butler." After watching the older gentleman cross the road, Maggie looked at her watch. There was just enough time to clean up before the skating party. She rose from the glider and went inside the house. Thirty minutes later, Reverend Jim rapped on the back door.

Helping Mary to the car, he said, "Monk's gone on ahead?"

"Yes," replied Mary. "He's picking up Dodie on his bike. I'm afraid you'll have to make do with motoring just Maggie and myself."

Reverend Jim smiled. "And I've never had the pleasure of such wonderful company." Maggie, catching the last bit of the conversation, slid into the vehicle's back seat and asked, "You'll be skating tonight, Reverend?"

"Yes, I believe I shall," he declared.

The local skating rink was on the outskirts of town. As Reverend Jim pulled the car into a parking spot, he waved at some of the church youth group members. "Have we all the supplies, Mary?" he asked before exiting the car.

"Yes, they should all have been delivered by now. Mr. Pratt is providing the paper and plasticware."

Opening Mary's car door, he continued, "Well then, shall we?"

"We shall," she replied. Maggie followed behind as Reverend Jim carefully escorted Mary into the building, and she said a quick prayer, grateful that Mary was healing so quickly.

A familiar disco tune was playing from the speakers as teenagers mingled throughout the large open space.

"It looks like they all showed up," said Reverend Jim.

"Oh, it would be pretty difficult to turn down a skating party," replied Maggie.

"How about I sit you here, Mary?" said the clergyman as he guided Miss Mary to a comfortable seat near the refreshments. "You'll have a pretty good view of the skating floor from here."

"This is fine. Thanks, Jim." Reverend Jim and Maggie went to the front counter, where Mr. Pratt handed each a pair of skates. They returned, sitting near Mary, and exchanged their shoes for skates. The clergyman was the first to finish lacing his skates.

"See you on the floor, Maggie!"

Maggie waved as Reverend Jim nimbly entered the skating area and mixed in with the crowd. She fiddled with her socks to alleviate the discomfort of the seams, then slipped on the skates. She carefully laced them up, making sure they felt just right. After receiving Mary's assurance that she was okay, Maggie skated onto the floor.

As she entered the circling crowd, the lights went out, and a large disco ball lit up in the middle of the floor, along with black lights around the room. A famous rock ballad reverberated from the speakers. After one lap of the rink, Maggie gracefully turned and began skating backward, lost in the music. Her white shirt, glowing purple from the black light, made it look like she was floating.

Reverend Jim, catching up with her, asked, "How about we show these youngsters how it's done?" Maggie smiled and nodded in agreement. He exited the rink to speak to Mr. Pratt and then returned as the song ended.

The two skated to the middle of the floor, pausing as the lights came up and the music changed. With the opening notes of a contemporary Christian song, they began a carefully choreographed routine. The teen skaters slowly rolled to a stop then began clapping along, eagerly watching the show. At the end of the song, loud applause filled the rink. Maggie and Reverend Jim politely took their bows then rolled off the floor.

"Where'd you learn to skate like that, Reverend Jim?" asked an astonished Tommy.

"Ah! That is what I did in my spare time in the Navy. I practiced skating on the ship deck, in port, on base, or wherever I had the time. I taught Maggie on a mission trip to West Germany."

Tired, the duo plopped down on the bench beside Mary. "'Be strong and courageous. Do not be afraid or terrified because of them, for the LORD your God goes with you; he will never leave you nor forsake you' (Deuteronomy 31:6)," Mary quoted. "What an excellent reminder that song is!"

Maggie smiled and grasped Mary's hand. "You are such an encouragement to me. I thank God for you every day." Tears welled up in Maggie's eyes.

"Now that's enough of that. This is a celebration. God has blessed us abundantly, and he makes us strong and courageous."

"Speaking of strength," interjected Reverend Jim, "how about a nice hot slice of cheese pizza, Mary? You need to eat to keep up your strength."

"Please and thank you. But as our Lord once told his disciples, 'I have food to eat that you know nothing about'" (John 4:32). Maggie and Reverend Jim smiled and hugged her.

Maggie watched the youth enjoying the skating party. There were so many different stories in that room, and God had written each one in a unique way. Would they indeed be strong and courageous, ready to take each adventure God had written for them?

Oh Father, I pray for these young people, your children. Teach them your way. Please give them the courage to hold to your teachings, even when the world laughs at them. Please help them to look beyond the temporariness of this world. Let them understand the eternal nature of your kingdom. Thank you for strength and victory in this mission. And thank you for the people you have placed in my life. I love you. In Jesus' name. Amen.

Very soon, she would be en route to the next mission. She didn't know what adventure awaited her in the arid and beautiful Chihuahuan Desert. For now, however, Maggie paused to thank God for his love and amazing plan for her life.

About
Kharis Publishing:

Kharis Publishing, an imprint of Kharis Media LLC, is a leading Christian and inspirational book publisher based in Aurora, Chicago metropolitan area, Illinois. Kharis' dual mission is to give voice to under-represented writers (including women and first-time authors) and equip orphans in developing countries with literacy tools. That is why, for each book sold, the publisher channels some of the proceeds into providing books and computers for orphanages in developing countries so that these kids may learn to read, dream, and grow. For a limited time, Kharis Publishing is accepting unsolicited queries for nonfiction (Christian, self-help, memoirs, business, health and wellness) from qualified leaders, professionals, pastors, and ministers. Learn more at: https://kharispublishing.com/